s m nostrini

PLANTAGENET TRILOGY - BOOK ONE

COURTNEY'S KEYS

UNLOCKING THE SECRETS OF THE HEART

Ark House Press
PO Box 1722, Port Orchard, WA 98366 USA
PO Box 1321, Mona Vale NSW 1660 Australia
PO Box 318 334, West Harbour, Auckland 0661 New Zealand
arkhousepress.com

Disclaimer: This is a work of fiction, names, characters, events and incidences are
either the products of the author's imagination or used in a fictitious manner.
Any resemblance to actual persons living or dead, or actual events is purely coinci-
dental. The town of Mt Barker and surrounding districts are real.

Cataloguing in Publication Data:
Title: Courtney's Keys: Book 1 Plantagenet Trilogy
ISBN: 978-0-6487607-3-3 (pbk)
Subjects: Christian Fiction; Historical Romance;

Design by initiateagency.com

for my cousins

Lynette Urbanski (dec), Susan Blaney-Murphy,

Carol Head and Janice Bennett

ACKNOWLEDGEMENTS

Thank you to my dear friends: Audrey Payne, Sharron Wise and Alison Inglis for your support, encouragement and time spent proofing and suggestions that have helped to bring this novel to fruition. I appreciate you all, and the friendship we share. May you be blessed by the plans our God has prepared for you.

My appreciation is extended to Bishop Ian Coutts, Anglican Diocese of Bunbury and Rev. Esther Leach, All Saints Anglican Church in Mt Barker for permission to include the churches of Southern Ranges Anglican Parish within the fictitious stories of The Plantagenet Trilogy.

It has been a pleasure to work with Nicole, James, John and the team from Initiate Media to produce this book. Thank you and God bless you all.

All Bible verse references are taken from the New International Version.

I would like to acknowledge the Noongar Menang people on whose land this book was written.

CHAPTER 1

Mt Barker, Western Australia
March, 1980

A rain-splashed Holden Commodore pulled up at the kerb. The passenger got out of the car and left the door ajar. She stood on the concrete footpath beside a paperbark tree; her eyes were fixed straight ahead, taking in the quaint weatherboard cottage. It looked sad, forlorn almost, not unloved but a little neglected. *I have an inheritance, me, Courtney.* The thunk of the taxi's boot as it closed, and the clunk of the door as it shut behind her registered in the corridors of her mind. But still, she stood looking, absorbed in her own world of thought.

"That'll be $55 please."

"Oh, yes, of course." She shook her head, pulled out a Billabong purse from her glossy vinyl handbag and gave him a $50 and $10 note. "Keep the change."

In the rear-view mirror the cab driver observed a solitary, slender young woman with long ash-blonde hair that hung halfway down her back. He drove off leaving her on the footpath with the battered suitcase beside her. *Strange girl,* he thought, and turned on the vacant light.

Courtney checked the address written on the envelope. Yes, it was right – 16 Lancaster Street, Mt Barker, Western Australia. The envelope in Courtney's hand had taken a bruising; it was dog-eared, and discoloured from where she'd rubbed her index finger over the contents during the taxi ride. She opened it carefully and took out an old-fashioned brass key tied to a faded red ribbon.

Blistered paint flaked from the pipe and wire gate that hung crookedly on its fence post. Rose beds flanked the central grey concrete path that led up to a set of rickety wooden steps. Tall wild oats waved in the breeze between thorny canes bearing dried rose-hips. Remnants of small red or white flowers clung tenaciously to their weak shoots. It might not be a grand mansion, but to Courtney having a home of her own was something she believed would only ever exist in her imagination. It didn't matter that it was on the other side of the country; it was hers.

She'd flown four uneventful hours from Sydney's Kingsford Smith International Airport to Perth. After a tedious wait in the airport reading a magazine and doing the crossword puzzle, Courtney boarded the afternoon flight to Albany. Landing 400 kilometres south an hour and a half later at the country airport, a light shower of rain greeted the passengers as they walked across the tarmac to the terminal. The sun shone through the grey sky and exhibited an impressive rainbow displaying its full spectrum of colour in pastel hues. It occurred to her that maybe this was all just a pot of unreachable gold and she would end up dealing with another disappointment in her life.

A damp Courtney collected her baggage and found a taxi right outside the exit doors. The driver was pleased she wanted to go to Mt Barker. It was only half an hour away and visitors to the region usually hired a car to travel around. He didn't mind; it would be a reasonable fare and he knew a bit about the town's history.[1] Courtney didn't take any notice of the information as her mind kept going over and over the interview with the lawyer in Sydney two days before.

"Come in, Miss Lancaster. I'm Jacob Hoyle." He put his hand out and offered her a firm handshake. The short man in his charcoal grey Armani suit, crisp white button-through shirt and wide lavender tie asked her to sit in the stylish black leather seat. He sat on a matching chair behind the desk and twiddled his thumbs. He looked directly into her eyes and she half expected him to apologise that she'd been dragged in here by a private investigator.

The PI was a big man with official credentials and a letter for her to prove he was legitimate. He'd insisted on escorting her to the office of Hoyle and Hoppman in Pitt Street. Courtney was afraid of the consequences if she didn't. Was it all a big mistake? Hoyle looked grim, although not unkind. His neat moustache twitched this time when he began to speak.

"Miss Lancaster, you are the beneficiary of your great uncle, Geoffrey Lancaster's will. It's not a wealthy man's estate you've inherited, but you'll be comfortable enough for a time I would think." He paused and took a sip of water from a crystal glass on a polished black marble coaster.

"The difficulty has been in locating you, but here we are with a good result at last. We realised there was an error made with the spelling of your surname at the orphanage, and it wasn't until you applied for a full birth certificate and your driver's licence that we were able to follow up the connection." Courtney swallowed hard and wiped her sweaty hands on her jeans.

---

1 Mt Barker, history (see Afterword)

"How long have you been looking for me?"

"Ever since you were six-years-old. Your great uncle would not give up the search and he made arrangements before he died for it to continue until we found you. He would've been a happy man to know this day has come."

"I didn't know I had any relatives." She paused. "When did he die?"

"Three years ago, I'm sad to say. Poor fellow, he hung on as long as he could, but his tired old body couldn't last any longer. He was ninety-one."

"So if I'd applied for my driver's licence when I was 16 or 17 instead of after I turned 20 he would've still been alive," she mused. "Maybe I could've met him."

"Sadly, that's the truth. Why did you wait so long? Most young people want to learn to drive as soon as they can."

"At the time my job was night-fill at a supermarket near where I lived, and I walked the two blocks to work. I slept during the day, and if I needed to go somewhere on the weekend, I'd use public transport. I didn't need a car or have any money for one, but my, um, circumstances changed. That's when I had to get those documents from the court house."

The lawyer explained all the intricacies of the law and the trust fund. When she turned twenty-one the following year everything would be handed over to her full custody. Arrangements were made by the lawyer for a generous allowance to be automatically deposited into a new bank account every month. They booked a trip to Western Australia and paid the airfares on her behalf.

The gate creaked when she pushed it open. Courtney lugged her case up the steps. It was heavy because everything she owned was stuffed into it. A wide verandah had two old cane chairs and a round coffee table in the corner that would've been inviting once. Now spider webs were intricately woven beneath them, and they needed a good scrub. The weatherboard cottage had a small window on either side of the front door. There was an oxidised brass emblem of three lions stacked one on top of the other above an old twist style bell that sat in the centre panel.

She looked at the key in her hand, lifted it up and then decided to ring the bell, just in case somebody was there. Her thumb and index finger tried to turn the tiny handle, but it didn't work. *Of course not,* she thought, *everything needs fixing.* A fresh lick of paint would be a good place to start. The key slid into the slot and turned in the barrel easily to unlock the door. Just as well, otherwise, she'd be camping out on the verandah for the night.

The door needed a firm push to open it. A dimly lit passageway smelled musty, and it gave the house an eerie atmosphere. She left the case in the hallway and looked into each room until she reached the kitchen at the end. It all seemed clean and tidy inside, which was quite remarkable since her great uncle had died three years ago.

A knock on the back door made her jump. No-one would knock if they thought someone had broken in, so, had someone seen her? What was she supposed to do? She felt out of place and like she shouldn't be there. Her instinct was to run and hide, but where would she go? A key turned in the lock, and the door opened a bit.

'Yoo hoo!" A short, plump woman with a friendly face and greying hair pulled back into a ponytail at the nape of her neck poked her head into the kitchen. Her warm brown eyes took in the pale face before her.

"Courtney?" she smiled at her.

The younger woman was more puzzled than alarmed.

"How do you know who I am?" she asked, her suspicious eyes squinting.

"We've been waiting for you for a long time. I'm sorry to frighten you; I'm Millie. Your great uncle Geoffrey was my neighbour and friend for nearly thirty years. I say 'we', but I do mean just 'me' because I've been waiting for you ever since he went to be with the Lord. It's good to see you."

How weird, this is all a bit much, but I suppose she's nice enough, she thought.

Millie came in with a jug of fresh milk and a plate of homemade biscuits.

"Let's put the kettle on and make a cup of tea. I expect you have a lot of questions you'd like answered. Today is such a grand day. How I wish dear Geoffrey was here. Never mind, he's in a better place, and I'm sure he's looking down from heaven and knows you're back where you belong. I'm thrilled for him, and I feel like I know you already."

Courtney couldn't believe the things this woman was saying; it seemed too far-fetched to be real.

Millie bustled around the kitchen efficiently finding cups and plates and spoons in a familiar manner. *She's done this before.* They pulled out chairs that scraped against the lino already worn from years of use and sat down. A sugar bowl, and a clear glass pepper and salt shaker with silver screw-top lids were on a doily in the centre of the green laminex and chrome table.

"Where should we start?" Millie stirred two spoons of sugar into her tea. Courtney didn't have any in hers, but put her elbow on the table and ran her fingers across her forehead. *Elbows off the table,* the mental reminder snapped at her, and she quickly put her hands down into her lap. Millie offered the plate of biscuits and Courtney took one. She was hungry. The oatmeal Anzac smelled and tasted delicious.

"I don't know ..." she looked around the room and shrugged her shoulders, "I'm confused." Many thoughts plagued her, and she honestly didn't know what to say.

"I've kept the place ready for you. The house needs a good airing, and that stale odour will go away. I don't like to leave the windows open when I'm not in here because you never know what might happen with the way things are in today's world." Millie waved her hand in the air as she spoke. *She doesn't look that old, probably sixty-something.*

"What was he like?"

"Oh, Geoffrey was the kindest man. Well, besides my Harold, of course. He was my husband, and we were married for forty years. Ten years ago he passed away, sad day that was. Only God knows why he took him before me. Anyway, about Geoffrey – he never married, but I know he had one true love because he'd sometimes talk about Matilda. He would get that faraway teary look in his eyes. I don't know what happened, but it broke his heart, whatever it was. Lived here by himself after he retired, he was an engineer, you know. Smart man and godly too, lived by the Good Book, he did. Bless him."

"Tell me, Courtney, what do you remember about your parents?"

That was from left field, and not where she wanted to go.

Yeah, and how many times have I been asked that?

"Not much, not much at all." End of conversation.

Millie caught her tone and tidied up. She waffled on about how the bed was made with fresh sheets, and clean towels were in the bathroom. It staggered Courtney to think she was expected to turn up one day. Fourteen years is a long time to wait for someone to come and knock on your door.

"You must be tired, and ready for a bath."

The chip heater for hot water had to be lit, and Millie showed her what to do. Newspaper, matches and kindling were in a bucket with some split wood.

"Be careful not to have too big a fire. The water can become scalding hot," Millie explained. "I'll bring some dinner over for you about 5.30ish. We'll have a chat tomorrow after you get some sleep."

The little lady went out the back door the same way she came in, but the key was left in the lock on the inside now.

CHAPTER 2

The bubble burst. Another one floated down and landed on the grass. It sat there and shimmered pink, blue and purple in the sunlight. A little girl with pigtails looked at her parents with a cheeky grin and gently poked the bubble. It burst, and she laughed out loud.

"Come on Mummy and Daddy, let's play the swinging game!"

Her parents took one hand each and held on with a firm grip.

"One, two, three - swing; one, two, three - swing."

The little girl's feet lifted off the ground, and she felt like she was flying through the air. She loved this game.

"Let's do it again," she giggled.

This time she landed on the ground with a thud, the imaginary bubble burst and her faceless Mummy and Daddy disappeared. She reached out, but there was no-one there to hold her hand and make her feel safe. They were gone, and she couldn't find them.

Courtney woke up; moisture stained the pillow where she'd been crying in her sleep. The dream was back again. She thought it was locked away in the recesses of her mind and couldn't escape, but Millie's question yesterday had dragged it out. If only she could remember something, anything, about her parents, then that dream couldn't keep haunting her.

It had been a restless night's sleep. The bed was uncomfortable. There was no traffic noise, no neon lights and no sirens, but strange unfamiliar noises disturbed her. When she finally fell into a deep slumber, the dream had come, and she couldn't go back to sleep. A cup of tea might help.

Courtney got up, put on her dressing gown and slippers to ward off the autumn chill, and went into the kitchen. She rummaged around to find the things she needed and tried to remember where Millie had put the teapot. There was only loose leaf tea, not teabags. The early morning sun crept over the horizon and lightened the sky, it was a new dawning for Courtney, *in many ways,* she thought, while she sipped her hot tea in the old-fashioned teacup. *I have a new beginning, and I'm going to make the most of it,* she decided.

The double hung timber window sashes were a bit stiff, but with a gentle force they opened and let in the fresh air and morning sunshine. The rooms looked much brighter with the blinds rolled up, and a cool breeze chased away that distinct odour to make the house appear much more homely than at her first observation.

There was a presence about the place, a positive one, but she couldn't put her finger on what it was. Courtney smiled, it was a good feeling to have your own house, and she would make it into the home she'd always longed for. Millie had given her some bread and butter, a jar of homemade marmalade and some Vegemite for breakfast when she delivered a delicious serve of shepherd's pie for dinner last night.

What a gem of a woman and Courtney couldn't help but like her. She was generous and kind, not at all nosy like she'd first thought.

A loud knock at the back door alerted Courtney to find Millie standing on the doorstep bearing a box of pantry items to stock the kitchen.

"I hope you don't mind, but I thought you could use these bits and pieces. The Co-op isn't open on Sunday, and the corner store prices are much more expensive. I only use it if I desperately need something. I'm off to church now, love, and I'll be home about midday if you need anything else."

Courtney put the food away in the cupboard and fridge, and then decided to explore the garden out the back. A Hills hoist clothesline stood sentinel in the middle of a grassed area with an old tin peg box attached to the post. Silvered wooden pegs were still in it. An overgrown veggie patch had once been productive judging from the rich soil and huge weeds, and an old timber and wire chook pen had housed chickens in a past life.

There was a shed down the back with a rusty padlock closed tight refusing access into its dark interior. It probably had an old lawnmower, rake and shovel in it. Courtney pulled a few weeds out of the vegetable plot and then got inspired to clear it all. An hour later a pile of dandelion, weeds and grass was stacked off to one side of the garden bed. Her hands were dirty with grit underneath her fingernails, but it felt good. She scrubbed up and made a sandwich. *I might attack that table and chairs out the front after lunch, and then I'd like to sit there in the afternoon sun.*

The front yard looked untidier than the back, but Courtney was too tired to do anything about it. She was exhausted after the trip across the country, a bad night, and the emotional turmoil going on in her head and heart. Millie was impressed when she saw the cleaned up table and chairs on the front verandah later in the day.

"I'm sorry about the garden being a bit of a mess, Courtney. It's just been too much for me to cope with recently. I arranged for a home maintenance man to mow the lawns and do the weeding but he's been away. I think he's due back next week. I'll make sure he comes to do it for you." Millie stirred her tea.

Courtney agreed that was a good idea, and asked if he would be able to do some repairs as well. Of course, Millie was sure that could be arranged. His name was Todd, of Yorkie's Home Help, and she had his card on the fridge.

It was just eight o'clock on Monday morning when a red Holden ute with a trailer of garden implements pulled into the driveway. A young man with long blonde hair hanging in his eyes jumped out and unloaded the rotary lawnmower. Courtney heard a car door close and the buzz of grass being cut while she was out the back hanging washing on the line. *It would be good of you to let me know you were here, mister,* she thought. However, it did occur to her that he would be unaware of an occupant being in the house because Millie wouldn't have had a chance to contact him yet. *I suppose I'd better go and introduce myself.*

"Are you Todd?" she approached him while he was bent over pulling the grass catcher off. He stood up, and smiled. It was difficult to know who got the biggest surprise. Courtney had felt uneasy at the vision of a surfie in jeans and singlet pushing the mower around the front yard. She'd expected a weathered old man with a bit of a paunch instead of the self-assured young fellow with vivid blue eyes and Colgate toothpaste commercial smile. Maybe this was his son, or someone else that worked for Yorkie's Home Help.

"Well, hello,' he drawled. "Yes, I am, and who might you be?"

"I'm the new owner, Courtney Lancaster. I'm hoping you might be able to do some work on the house for me. Millie said you do that sort of thing as well as gardening."

"I don't see why not," his eyes lingered on her face and then he looked her up and down.

"Don't see any reason why I can't, not at all."

She noticed his assessment of her, but ignored it.

"Can you give me a quote to repair the front gate and steps? And if you do painting, I'd like to have the house repainted as well. There might be other things that need fixing as you go."

"Sure thing, it might take a while." His eyes looked over the house and back at Courtney.

"The painting, that is, not the quote. I could be here for a while, yes, quite a while."

His eyes looked straight through her, almost like as if he knew her, like she didn't want him to know.

Millie was on her knees beside the bed with her Bible open at the Old Testament book of Jeremiah, Chapter 29.

"Thank you, Lord, for bringing Courtney here. I'm concerned though, Lord, that I don't have the right words to say to her. She's got a wall wrapped around herself, and you know what's caused that and the journey she's had up til now. I don't want to let her down, and I have to trust your word, Lord, that you know the plans you have for her. It's not for me to understand what they are, but you know the end from the beginning. I trust you to lead and guide me to help her."

Millie spent a long time praying, and her knees were sore when she got up off the carpet mat on the polished wooden floorboards. She tucked a strand of hair behind her ear and smiled. That felt better. It was always good to come before the Lord with the burden of one's heart.

She heard a lawnmower going outside that she hadn't noticed before. *Oh, good, Todd must be next door.* The flywire door banged shut as she went out the back. *Maybe I can get him to fix that door closer for me, as well.* Millie walked up the path to the side gate that connected the two homes. Geoffrey had it put in after Harold died in case either of them needed help in a hurry. She caught the look on young Todd's face when he was speaking to Courtney. It bothered her, so she interrupted their conversation.

"Todd, I'm glad to see you. I was going to get in touch this week."

"Hello, Millie."

The young man's attitude shifted.

"How was your holiday? Where did you go again?"

A genuine smile lit his face.

"I had a great time surfing in Indonesia. They've got wicked surf there, and a lot of really hot chicks."

"That'll be enough of that talk," Millie chided, scowling at him.

"Sorry."

An insincere apology, but nevertheless, it was done out of respect for her.

"So, have you had a chance to talk about the house?"

"Yes, I'm going to give a quote for what she wants done."

"Courtney, you mean, not 'she'. Excellent, and can you please have a look at my back door for me while you're at it?"

"Okay. I haven't got time to do anything about it today. I have to catch up on all the lawns that need mowing, but I'll be in touch soon."

He looked at Courtney when he made the last part of the statement. *Yeah, and I'm not going to be able to get away with much with the old biddy next door keeping an eye on things.* Todd was disappointed with that realisation.

Millie and Courtney sat on the top verandah step and watched Todd load the mower onto the trailer. He saluted a wave toward them as he drove off. They looked at each other and started laughing.

"Thanks for saving me from him," Courtney said casually, although she meant it.

"He's pretty harmless, mostly, I think, but he's not keeping good company lately. I've known that young man since he was a child and he's not a bad boy."

She hoped he wasn't, but people can change when they make wrong choices, and she was well aware of that.

"Now, let me tell you some things Geoffrey wanted you to know."

"The lawyer already did that."

"No, I mean more personal things."

The older woman spoke to Courtney about her great uncle Geoffrey's faith in God, and how he longed for her to know about

Jesus, and salvation and forgiveness. Courtney had blamed God for taking her parents away from her and leaving her at the mercy of people who didn't care. She wasn't too happy about the idea of having to listen to all this stuff either, but because she'd been the only beneficiary of her great uncle's money and property she owed it to him to hear Millie out.

"Geoffrey wanted you to have the freedom to do what you want with his possessions because they're yours now and you can choose to do whatever you like with it all."

Millie left her with an assurance that she was available for anything at any time, and all she needed to do was ask. Then she went home.

The wicker basket held her freshly laundered clothes. Courtney put it on the kitchen table while she considered which room she would use as her own. The one she'd stayed in for the last two nights was small with a single bed, and she didn't want to use it again tonight. The sleep-out on the back verandah would probably be cold in winter, so she didn't want to use that either. That left the main bedroom, Geoffrey's room. She timidly went in and looked at it in a different light to when she'd gone in there to open the window earlier.

The furniture was simple; a dark timber bedroom suite consisted of a double bedstead, two bedside tables, a wardrobe, and a dressing table with three drawers and a mirror. There wasn't a speck of dust on any of it because Millie had kept it clean. The floor was carpeted but quite worn on one side where it was most used. She ran her hand over the faded light blue chenille quilt. *Yes, this can be my room.*

The folded underwear fitted into the top drawer neatly, pyjamas went in the second drawer and jumpers were in the third one. One bedside table drawer held bits and pieces she wanted to put away for now. Dresses, pants, shirts, and skirts would have to go into the wardrobe, and she hoped there were coat hangers in it. She didn't have a lot of clothes, and never had done. At the Home they were only allowed two of everything, except undies because they were given four of them.

A brown key sat in the keyhole of each wardrobe door. She unlocked the left door, and it swung open. There were quite a lot of coat hangers in there. She hung her clothes and wondered if there might be some shelves on the right-hand side for her jeans. She preferred to fold them. Courtney opened the other door, and there were shelves, but they had parcels on them.

She pulled one out; it had a card taped to the top of it. 'Courtney' was written on the envelope. *What ...?* She pulled out another one, and it was the same. They were all for her. She couldn't believe it. The gifts sat on the bed, five neatly wrapped presents with ribbon ties, and five cards by themselves without gifts and one parcel that hadn't been wrapped very well with no card. Maybe there was another Courtney that they were for, surely they weren't for her. *I'll just unwrap one and see what's in there. There could be a clue to the puzzle in the card.*

> Dear Courtney,
> Wishing you a very Happy Birthday
> May God bless you every day,
> with love and prayers from Gr.uncle Geoff.

The card was pink with a glittery number 6 and a pretty girl sitting on a tree swing with a kitten curled up on her lap. It was for her, for her sixth birthday, and she'd never received it. There was one for when she was seven, and eight, nine and ten. All beautiful cards, but the messages grew each year. They said things like, 'missing you, looking for you, hoping to find you soon ...'. They were all signed Gr.uncle Geoff, in his small but strong handwriting. Disbelief filled her thoughts, but it was true, they were meant for her.

The presents were a pink china piggy bank, a beanie and matching scarf, bangles and hair ribbons, a sewing box, and an array of pink, and blue and purple beads. The girl inside the young woman groaned with the love that was poured out upon her. A love she'd never felt before, ever. The envelopes held birthday cards with $50 notes and came with assurances that she could buy whatever she liked with the money. It was hers, and her choice to spend it how she wanted.

Scripture verses were hand-written in the cards, but only the book of the Bible, chapter and verse, and not the words. She didn't know what they would say. *Millie might help me to find out what they are, when I'm ready, which I'm not yet.* Fifty dollars would have been a lot of money to give a girl between the age of eleven to sixteen, and the notes were crisp new ones. Courtney made a stack of the $50 notes beside the pile of cards and shook her head. The gift with no name left her bewildered. Should she open it, or should she leave it?

Sitting on the floor with the parcel in front of her, Courtney noticed that the sticky tape was doubled up in some places, and scrunched in others. The brown paper didn't quite meet in some spots, and it was tied up with string to hold it together. It was intriguing, and she couldn't resist pulling the bow undone. Carefully peeling the paper away, and slowly unravelling the gift, she discovered a cross-stitch sampler in an antique wooden frame; the alphabet and numbers were surrounded by a border of white roses. There was also a tattered dark blue box. She found a gold heart-shaped locket and some notepaper folded in quarters with two keys inside it.

That might explain the mystery; it was for her and written in Gr.uncle Geoff's handwriting dated 1st July, 1977. It was hard to read, not neat and strong, and some of it was scrawled across the page in spider-like fashion.

> Dear Courtney,
>
> This gift, unlike the others, is not new. I've always wanted to give it to you for Christmas, and it's very special to me. I have saved it up from one year to the next. That explains why I have birthday gifts for you, but there aren't any other presents for Christmas.
> I'm very old, and I don't think I'll be on this earth much longer. Matilda sewed the sampler. We fell in love, but because of her family's position in society and our different religious denominations, we were unable to marry. I gave her the locket before we were forced apart. I've treasured both of them since they were sent to me years ago. Tildy died when she was just 33.
> I have always wanted to find you and share our family history with you. I'm sorry we might not get the chance to reunite, but I want you to know you were loved immensely. The keys will unlock the trunk and the music box.
>
> Gr.uncle Geoff

A raw emotion roiled through her, and she felt distraught. *Reunited, but that means I had already met him or knew him once before.*

Courtney held the note in a shaky hand and the keys in the other. A gut-wrenching cry emanated from her throat, and she had no control over it. Grief and torment for a life that was lost bubbled up from deep within. She sobbed.

An hour later the young woman washed her face and brushed her hair, her eyes red and swollen. She had to keep blowing her nose, and tears continued to slip down her cheeks.

A trunk and a music box, where are they? What do they hold?

CHAPTER 3

Todd bound up the front steps of Courtney's house, and nearly tripped on a loose stair. He knocked on the door. No answer. He tried to ring the doorbell, but it was seized up. *That needs some attention. Just like the owner.* He smiled at this thought and waited, there was still no answer. *Maybe I should go around the back.* The door opened as he turned to walk away.

"Hi, I was beginning to think you weren't home."

"Sorry, I was busy with something."

She was distant.

"Are you okay?"

"Yeah, what do you want?"

No niceties there.

"I thought I'd drop off the quote for the painting. The gardening's already covered by bank payments every month, and unless that changes, we'll continue with it as it is. I see your doorbell needs fixing, and some of the steps need replacing. I can charge for those repairs as they pop up. Is that all right with you?"

Her demeanour was cool and unfriendly, and he knew she didn't want him there.

Courtney nodded and took the quote. She gave it a quick look. Preparation, some specified repairs and painting were included. She looked at him.

"When can you start?"

"Next week. I can be here bright and early on Monday morning." Todd smiled.

"Have you got paint charts, so I can pick the colours I want?"

"I can get some for you and drop them back."

"Yes, please." And she shut the door.

Todd just stood there. *That went well!*

Three weeks later he admired his workmanship. An aura of warm Winter White emanated from the weatherboards. Cleaning, sanding, cutting in and brushing resulted in a job well done, and he was pleased. The window frames, architraves and front door contrasted in their soft half-tint of slate grey. The house looked handsome. He thought so, but he had no idea what Courtney's opinion was. He hadn't seen her except for a few brief, cold-shouldered consultations over repairs that he ran by her before taking on the work. She wanted the costs to calculate the expenditure on the renovation.

The 27-year-old Todd had hated school. He wanted to be outside, and not cooped up in a classroom, but his father had insisted he finish his education, and because he had a bright mind he got through without too much effort. His Dad wanted him to go to university, but that's where he drew the line. Uni was not on the agenda for his future. It took some effort, but he managed to arrange an apprenticeship as a carpenter with a builder in town who taught him far more about building than working with wood. He finished his four years of training and worked for the company for a couple of years before going out on his own. He liked the freedom to drive to Albany beaches for an hour or two of surfing when the waves were pumping. He wasn't obliged to work from nine-to-five for someone else or have to fake a 'sickie' to escape. Todd recalled the conversation he'd had with Millie the day before when he fixed her back door closer. They shared the same concerns over her next door neighbour.

"Millie, have you spoken to Courtney recently. I'm not getting anywhere with her, and I don't mean in a flirty kind-of-way either. I backed off weeks ago because I got the message loud and clear that she was a no-go zone. Has she talked to you about what's going on?"

"Oh, dear. No, I haven't been to visit her because of all the work you were doing, and I thought she was too busy."

"When I saw her on Monday morning she looked pale and thin. I don't think she's in a good place."

Millie's eyes filled with tears.

"Oh, Toddy ..."

"Please don't call me that."

"Sorry, I forgot; old habit. I've neglected her, and I promised Geoffrey I'd take care of her. I should've gone over, but I didn't want to be pushy."

"She's a grown woman, Millie. You don't have to feel guilty."

"But she's had it tough, Todd, and I want to be there for her. I'd better get praying and work out what to do."

Ever the Christian, Todd thought. But he had to admire the old woman for her faithfulness. That was something he'd forgotten about in recent years.

"Well, you'd better start soon, 'cos I have to deliver my final invoice tomorrow. I'd like the chance to actually talk to her, you know, properly and not get a short change conversation."

Todd felt nervous, and that wasn't like him when it came to lovely young ladies. Courtney had knocked his ego off-kilter. *I hope Millie's doing her praying thing.* Millie had been fasting and praying since he'd left the day before for both of them.

The doorbell rang loud and clear. Todd smiled. *That's a good start.* Well, he hoped it was. The door opened wide, and Courtney invited him in. *Even better.*

He paused at the threshold, and she noticed his hesitance.

"Come in, and I promise I won't bite." A half-smile hinted upon her lips. "I know I've been rude, and I apologise," and with that said, an element of his confidence returned.

Todd strode down the passageway to the kitchen behind her. *She looks good from here, too.* Then he scolded himself for thinking like that. *I'd better get those thoughts under control because she'll know. She's good at reading my mind.* They sat at the kitchen table, and he gave her the bill.

"I hope you're satisfied with the job, Courtney."

He looked at her with hopeful eyes, and her frosty cage began to melt a bit more.

"Satisfied? You're an excellent tradesman, and the house looks amazing. I love it."

That was a relief, and he relaxed.

"I'll get the cheque book."

As she walked out of the room Todd's thoughts wandered again. She returned, wrote out and signed a cheque, and slid it across the table to him.

"Thanks, its good timing. I'll need that for when I go across to Margaret's at Easter."

"Where does she live?"

"Not 'she', it's where - Margaret River. There are plenty of surf breaks along the coastline, and I can't wait to get into a barrel and ride a wave. Best surf in Western Australia."

"So what language is that? Surf talk, I suppose, and it means nothing to me."

Todd got excited and explained what it all meant and more. She listened without enthusiasm, her grey eyes clouded over and he noticed her lack of interest.

"I'm a good listener, not only a talker, you know," he stated softly.

She tilted her head a little and apologised again.

"It's okay, but I admit I'm a bit worried. I know something's bothering you and if you want to talk about it, I'm here, anytime."

There was a pregnant pause in the conversation. He waited. She fidgeted and tears blurred her vision. He reached out and gently touched the back of her hand. She pulled it away, but her resolve left her, and the tears spilled over.

"I don't know how to deal with all this stuff," she whispered hoarsely.

Todd could only just hear what she'd said. He waited some more.

"So many emotions I've never felt before. It's all a bit overwhelming."

Courtney let out a breath through puffed cheeks. *Maybe it would be good to talk to someone, but is Todd the right person?* He was here, and he was being kind. All of her defences were down.

"I want to go and get some things to show you. Is that all right?" she asked.

"Of course it is." *Be careful, Todd, she's fragile. Don't mess this up and make things worse.*

Courtney placed her bundle on the table and spread the gifts out. He wasn't sure what it all meant, but she explained about finding them in the cupboard.

"How thoughtful of him, we all knew he was searching for you."

"You did! How come?"

Surprise lit her eyes, lightening them to a blue tinge.

"Small town, everybody knows everyone and everything that goes on in this place."

"Oh, really?"

She was used to knowing what went on at the Home. It hadn't occurred to her that a whole town would share personal details with other people.

"Yep. It's hard to keep secrets, but occasionally it's possible."

Todd raised his eyebrows.

"Are you speaking from experience?"

"Not my own," he shook his head.

Maybe she could trust him.

Todd lifted the beads up and held them out to her.

"Go on, put them on."

"That's a silly idea."

"No, it's not. They're yours, and you never got to wear them when you were a kid. Here."

He placed them over her head. She smiled and flicked her hair out at the back. The bangles went on as well. They both laughed when the beanie fit tight to her scalp. It was only just big enough. When Courtney opened out the scarf she found a pair of gloves. They were definitely too small. She half put one on, with loose knitted fingers flapping around.

"Hah, looks like a rooster with its head chopped off."

They chuckled at the idea of the image it portrayed. Todd picked up the pink china piggy bank and turned it over.

"No plug in the bottom. That's a shame."

He shook it. Coins rattled within, he tipped it upside down and began to shake it gently with expert skill.

"What are you doing?" Courtney was puzzled.

"Getting the money out," he carefully grabbed a five cent coin poking through the slot and pulled it out. "You don't want to smash your piggy do you?"

"It's supposed to be used to save money, isn't it?"

"Yeah, but sometimes you need to have a bit to spend on lollies." His cheeky smile stretched across his face. "I used to be very good at doing this. I had plenty of practice until they started making money boxes with an opening in the bottom. It was easy to get your money out then."

The doorbell rang. Courtney pulled the glove off and went to answer the door.

"Hi, Millie. Why didn't you come to the back door?"

"I couldn't open the gate and carry the cake as well."

She stood there with a strawberry decorated cream sponge layer cake on a pretty china plate.

"Can you manage some more company? Otherwise, take the cake and share it with Todd. Although, I'd like some, I feel a bit peckish."

"Come in, please."

"I see you found your presents," Millie stated.

Courtney rolled her eyes, she'd forgotten about the beads and beanie. She pulled the knitted cap off her head. *It seems like they know more about me than I know about myself.*

The kettle was on, and the knife cut through the feather-light cake easily, but Courtney didn't know what to do next. She tried to lift the cake to put it on a side plate, but the top half lost its balance and fell off. Embarrassed, she tried to pick it up again, and it plopped in a mess on the plate. She looked at Millie with a pleading glance for help.

"Would you like me to serve for you?" Millie came to her rescue. Courtney nodded, relieved at her neighbour's suggestion. The threesome enjoyed their afternoon tea together, and then Todd left.

The two women collected the dishes from the table and went to the kitchen sink.

"Do you want to wash, or wipe up?" Millie asked.

"I'll wipe, I had to wash thousands of dishes in the Home. It's my pet hate."

Courtney smiled at Millie who had her hands in the hot water and dishwashing suds in no time.

"Millie, can I ask you how you knew those things were presents for me?"

"Of course, you can. Geoffrey took me shopping to help him find a suitable gift each year. He hoped you would be there to open it yourself, and was disappointed when it had to be put away again." Tears filled her eyes at the memory of his sadness. She glanced at Courtney who had begun to cry.

"Oh, sorry, I can't believe I've become such a cry-baby blubbering all the time. I don't remember being reduced to tears while I was growing up. I think I must've put a big barrier around my heart after I was told about my parents."

"That's not surprising. What a terrible shock you would've had. You were so young to be left alone." Millie was being careful with her words.

"Gr.uncle Geoff, that's how he signed the cards."

"I didn't know what he wrote in them, that's lovely. He always picked out the cards himself, you know."

"I had no idea someone actually loved and cared about me. Just being here and discovering all of this makes me very emotional." Millie wiped her hands on the towel and put her arms out. Courtney accepted the embrace, although she was a little stiff and not quite sure what to do.

The gifts on the table had been pushed over to one side. Courtney caressed them before she put them away. The piggy bank sat on the mantle over the stove and the other things were arranged on the dressing table in her room. The coin still sat on the table because she hadn't put it back in the money box.

When Courtney wiped the laminex top to clear off the cake crumbs she picked it up. It shone brightly. Something caught her attention, it was the date – 1966, a newly minted decimal currency coin. She sat down, her legs felt weak and her hands were shaking. A memory exploded in her mind.

A sixpence and a five-cent coin on Valentine's Day! Daddy had bought red roses for Mummy and a shiny coin for her. It all came flooding back.

"But I don't want that one," a stubborn pig-tailed Courtney whined. Her parents had picked her up from school and she was still in her uniform.

"Courtney, this is the new money that Australia is going to use from now on," her father explained. "See the echidna on the back of it, it's very cute. Just like you," he smiled.

"I don't care. I want a sixpence instead."

She folded her arms and refused to take the gift.

"Why? I don't understand why you're making such a fuss."

"Because the sixpence is worth more, see, that's only got a five on it – not a number six."

Daddy looked over the top of her head to see a slow smile grow on his wife's face.

"Well, of course, Daddy. Was it not you who told her the difference between a half-penny, a penny, a threepence and a sixpence?"

The man sighed, yes, he had. He took his daughter on his knee and gave her a hug.

"Okay, so you need to know that we are not going to use those other coins anymore. If you take them to the bank, the sixpence and five-cent coin are the same value now."

"Can I have the shiny one and still buy the same lolly bag from the corner shop?"

"Yes, and we can go and do that on the way home after we finish our cup of coffee and you drink your lemonade."

"All right," Courtney beamed. Lemonade and lollies on the same day, that was love all wrapped up in one.

Courtney closed her eyes and shook her head when she realised that this had really happened. She remembered it clearly now, it was a happy day. She smiled to herself. She could picture her parents, what they looked like and how their voices sounded. At last, she had something to hold on to. She ran next door excited to share the memory. *I have to go and tell Millie, I have to tell somebody.*

CHAPTER 4

I t happened again, she had another flashback. Courtney was
enveloped in the warm memory of going to school in Perth. Her
mother would hold her hand as they walked to the Grade One
classroom. She helped to hang her school bag on a hook and then
put her arms out to her daughter. "Give me a quick hug, and then
you can play with your friends," she would say. Unspoiled happiness
flooded Courtney's mind as she recalled the daily ritual.

She welcomed the memories. Her parents were an attractive
couple. Her father had been tall with sandy coloured hair and a
reddish beard. Her mother was tiny by comparison; her dark hair
was just long enough to sit on her shoulders. It shone in the sunlight.
Courtney couldn't recall the colour of their eyes or any other
significant feature, but it didn't matter. Remembering these snippets
had opened a sliver of attachment she had long ago forgotten.

The birthday cards had been sitting on the sideboard in the lounge
room for several weeks. The bench needed dusting and it was time to
put them away. Reluctantly, Courtney collected them and went to put
them in the other bedside table drawer. An old black leather Bible sat
in there by itself.

Picking it up, she noticed worn gold lettering on the bottom right-hand corner of the cover. It looked like CLL, her initials, Courtney Louise Lancaster. The name inside was written in traditional black ink calligraphy: Geoffrey Louis Lancaster. Ah, so the hook on the G was rubbed off and looked like a C. The young woman smiled, yet another connection.

Maybe she could use the Bible to look up those verses in the cards. It intrigued her to find out what they said, and although she wasn't sure how to do it she could work it out by using the index. That might be better than asking Millie. It would save her from any deep and meaningful discussions. They did have a Bible at the Home, but it was rarely used and sat on a shelf collecting dust except for Christmas Day when it was taken down to read the story of when Jesus was born. She had loved to hear about the angels and shepherds, and the wise men.

The last card Uncle Geoff gave her had the reference Jeremiah 29:11-14. Courtney sat on the bed and opened the Bible. She checked the index for the book of Jeremiah and found the page. Turning the thin pages she looked for the large number 29, there it was, and it was easy to find the verses because they'd been coloured-in lightly with a red pencil.

It said, "I know the plans I have for you, plans to prosper you and not to harm you, plans to give you hope and a future. Then you will call on me and come and pray to me, and I will listen to you. You will seek me and find me when you seek me with all your heart. I will be found by you," declares the Lord, "and I will bring you back from captivity. I will gather you from all the nations and places where I have banished you," declares the Lord, "and will bring you back to the place from which I carried you into exile."

Is that what happened to me? Was I banished? Why would God do that to a little girl? What plans could He possibly have for me now?

All these confusing thoughts bounced around in Courtney's mind. She simply did not understand what it could mean and wondered why Uncle Geoff would put a verse like this in her card. Her eyes kept going back to the first line, plans to prosper, hope, a future, and she sensed peace about these words in spite of the unsettling sentences that followed.

On Monday morning the bank opened at 9.30am. Courtney needed to get some money out for grocery shopping. She walked down Lowood Road into town and turned into Langton Street. It was just 9.25am. An elderly lady and a gentleman were already there when she arrived. A young man came to open the doors and allowed the customers to enter the building. Courtney waited for her turn after the lady was served and passed her bank book and withdrawal slip across the counter.

"Can I have $100 cash, please?" she asked.

The teller looked at the form, checked her name and looked up at her.

"Just one moment, please, Miss." He turned and locked the cash drawer and left her standing there. She knew there was enough money in the account, so what was the problem?

"Um, Miss Lancaster, there seems to be an issue here." He'd returned to his counter. "I'm afraid the manager has frozen your account until further notice."

"What? Why?" She was stunned.

"Well, I can't tell you but if you would like to make an appointment to see the manager he will be able to explain."

"Yes, of course, I want to see him. When is he available?" She paused and then spoke again. "I want to see him right now."

Her voice had risen, and anxiety showed on her face. Other customers in the room were aware of what had transpired, and she was embarrassed.

"He's not available until after 10 o'clock. Do you want to wait or make an appointment for tomorrow?"

"I'll wait!"

Courtney was frustrated and wanted to find out what was going on today. She took her bank book back and sat on the chair by the door. The male customer glanced at her on his way out.

Great, now everybody in town will think I'm a fraud. They don't even know me yet. That's not a good start to my new life.

She fumed while she waited. Ten o'clock came and went and just before 11.15am the manager came out of his office and called her in. The sign on the door had his name written in capital letters – MR GORDON PRESCOTT and the line underneath read: WA Agricultural Bank - Manager. Courtney didn't care who he was, she was past being polite.

"Why can't I have my money?"

She stood in front of the desk that sat between them.

"Your account isn't available for you to access money from it."

The tall reed-thin balding man pushed back on his chair and directed an air of defiance toward her.

"So I've been told, but I want to know why and I want this sorted out now."

"No chance of that, Missy." He pointed his cigarette-stained index finger at her. "I'm not releasing any more funds out of Geoffrey Lancaster's account into yours until I've been given proof of your identity."

"But that's been arranged by the solicitor in Sydney."

"I don't know him, and I don't trust him any more than I trust you. You're not getting another cent from this bank while I'm here, Missy." His sarcastic word choice grated on her nerves.

"We'll see about that." Courtney walked out of the office and left the building.

Tears stung her eyes, and she worked hard to hold them back. She trudged home; it felt a lot further away than it had when she'd walked into town this morning. Her day had turned from bright sunshine into a big black cloud hanging over her head.

What am I going to do now? I'll have to use the money that Uncle Geoff gave me for my birthday presents. I wanted to keep them, I don't want to have to spend it.

She had no choice if she was going to eat this week. Her mind reeled with the options of what could be done, and to ring Sydney long-distance was expensive. She had to talk to Jacob Hoyle. He was the only person who would know what to do.

Todd was about to pull out of Courtney's driveway when he saw her walking down the road. He'd just cut the lawns and trimmed the edges at her place, and he sat in the car with the motor idling. Her face looked like thunder. Todd hesitated to stay but decided to wait for her to get within earshot.

"What's up?" he asked.

"I can't believe that bank manager. He's frozen my account and I can't get my money."

"Can he do that? I wouldn't have thought he'd have that sort of authority."

"Well, he has." She felt like swearing but restrained herself.

"I can help you out with some cash if you need it," Todd offered.

"Thanks, but I'll be all right. I have to contact the solicitor in Sydney to act on my behalf."

Todd looked past Courtney's shoulder, then back at her.

"Do you know who that is?" He indicated with his chin in the direction across the road. She glanced at the vehicle parked nearby.

"No, why?"

"It's just that he drove slowly behind you while you walked home."

Courtney visibly paled. Her body stiffened, and she stuttered her response.

"Wha...? Do you think ... do you mean I was followed?"

She swallowed around the nervous lump in her throat.

"Maybe, but I'm probably being suspicious for nothing." Todd's attitude changed.

"How about coming to Margaret River with me for the Easter break?" he asked tentatively. "I'm leaving on Thursday after lunch."

"No, thanks."

"Oh, come on, you'll have a good time. I'll make sure of it."

His face lit with anticipation.

"Absolutely not!" Courtney turned on her heel and walked away.

Todd forced the utility's accelerator down and roared off up the road with the trailer bouncing along behind, tools clattering as he went.

A distinguished-looking man in a suit and tie stepped out of his car after Todd drove away, and he spoke to Courtney briefly on her front verandah.

Todd was halfway home before his temper cooled and the realisation hit him that she might not be safe. That man in the car could be stalking her. Reluctantly, he turned the vehicle around and thought he'd better go back and check to make sure she was all right. The parked car was gone, and as he approached her house, he caught sight of her going through the back gate to Millie's.

Good, I won't worry now. I don't know why I'd bother to worry about her anyway.

He drove home, sullen, but shifted his thoughts to surfing on the weekend and put the whole thing behind him.

"Millie ... Hello." Courtney called out as she tapped on the flywire door. "Are you there?"

"Coming," Millie came down the passage and waved her in.

"What was all that noise about?" she asked.

Courtney shrugged.

"Just Todd being Todd."

"Oh, I see." Of course, Millie understood what she'd meant but had no idea what had transpired. "Do you want a cuppa?"

Courtney thought that might soothe her rattled state and agreed to a cup of tea. Her story of the trip to the bank poured out in a torrent while her tea sat untouched, and it was lukewarm by the time she swallowed the first mouthful. Millie was sympathetic and offered her financial assistance as well.

'I don't want to seem ungrateful, Millie, but I want to be independent. I'll manage until I have access to my account again. Thanks, anyway." She had been turning a business card over and over in her hands while they'd been talking. Courtney stopped and looked at it.

"Have you ever heard of Keith Crawford?" She read from the card.

"No, who is he?"

"He owns a vineyard at Frankland River. Crawford Estate Winery."

"How do you know him?"

Millie wondered where this was going.

"I don't, I only met him a few minutes ago. He was at the bank and heard everything. He's offered to help me out as well. That seems odd to me because he's a total stranger. Maybe he has an ulterior motive, although, he was friendly enough."

"Are you forgetting that we were total strangers not so long ago?" Millie smiled, and crinkles appeared at the corner of her ageing eyes. "How could he help you?"

"I'm not sure, but he told me to contact him if there was anything I needed." She tapped the corner of the card on the table. "I'll keep his number, just in case I decide I want to speak to him again."

Courtney rang Jacob Hoyle and left it up to him to solve the problem with the bank. He'd sounded confident it would be easy to fix.

CHAPTER 5

Todd loaded the back of the ute with a swag, his surfboard and other swimming gear. A box of fresh and tinned food, a can opener, frypan, matches and a primus gas burner were included in his packing for the weekend. He became more excited at the prospect of riding the waves than he had for some time. It's what he needed. He'd be able to release all that recent nervous tension and could catch up with some of the other guys that he only saw at the beach these days. The drive across to the coast was uneventful, which is a good thing when travelling along lonely country roads.

The red ute pulled into the campgrounds at Cowaramup Bay just north of Margaret River. The North Point reef break was out in the bay, and Todd was hopeful of a long, heavy right-hander to surf the next day. The sun had begun to lower in the western sky. The silhouette of a solitary yacht on the horizon contrasted to the reflection of golden rays that shimmered across the waves of the Indian Ocean.

Todd opened a can of baked beans and ate them cold straight out of the tin with a teaspoon, munched on a raw carrot and ate an apple. He climbed into the back of the ute, unrolled his swag and slept soundly ready to rise early on Good Friday morning.

Dawn broke, and a crisp chill in the air invigorated Todd's senses. He drank some water and squeezed into his wetsuit, pulled the rear zip cord up and made himself comfortable. Even though his face was tanned he dabbed sunscreen on his nose, cheeks and chin to protect them from sunburn.

Todd picked up his waxed surfboard, tucked it under his arm and jogged down the sandy track to the beach. Warmed up and feeling ready for the ride of his life he entered the water and paddled out. There were a few surfers in the line-up, and he sat on his board waiting for his turn. Then it came, and it was worth the wait. He charged into the hollow and rode the barrel, then he kicked out through the back of the wave.

Stoked, a grin stretched across his face, *yes, I want to do that again.* After a few hours Todd came out of the water, and stripped the wetsuit down to his waist before going back to camp to make a decent breakfast.

Ants tickled his nose and woke Todd from his slumber on the beach towel where he'd fallen asleep in the shade of the melaleuca trees. He'd dreamed of Courtney sitting out the back on a surfboard, all his hopes dashed when she wiped-out and screamed at him that she was not the girl for him. *I wasn't going to think about her,* but his subconscious wouldn't let her go. She was still on his mind. He pushed those random thoughts aside.

"Hey, dude. Haven't seen you since Indo. How's it goin'? Wade asked Todd when he saw him standing near his vehicle brushing ants off his shoulder.

"Yeah, all right. You?"

"Yeah, you been to Yallingup recently? It's pumpin' huge pipes. We came down south to check out what's offering. Wanna get together tonight, we're down the track a bit. Just follow the noise, that's where you'll find us."

"Okay, see you then."

"Oh, and bring your own beer. We don't wanna share ours." Wade laughed and took off.

After reading the wind and the waves, it looked good for an awesome late afternoon session in the surf. Hungry after all the intense physical exertion, Todd cooked up a substantial meal and devoured it. He showered and put on clean board shorts and a tank top before he wandered off to find Wade and his mates.

"Yo bro, you're here." They made a space for him around the campfire and popped the cap off another beer. Todd had his own stash and made short work of it in a couple of hours. He didn't get back to the ute that night, just crashed where he was and woke up with a thumping headache and felt sick. Feeling like that doesn't make for a good day of surfing.

Todd went down to the beach to check out the conditions, but the waves were closing out, and there was a lot of whitewash. Bikini-clad, suntanned girls lazed on the golden sand. He glanced across at the surf chicks and it wasn't long before there was a bevy of beauties around him laying it on thick with their compliments. He soaked it all in, his ego blossomed at their words and thrilled at their hands running over his lithe body.

One girl, Freya, hung around him all day and invited him to a party in Margaret River where her family had a holiday house. It used to belong to her grandparents. No-one other than the partygoers would be there, she assured him. Not that he cared, he was way older than she was and probably her friends as well. *Why not?* He convinced himself that he was due for a good time.

The afternoon had a change in the wind direction, and the waves were cranking. Todd went for it and nearly didn't bother with the party invitation. *Oh, hang it,* he decided he'd go anyway. It was crowded, loud music rattled the windows, and the grog flowed. Freya latched onto him when she realised he'd turned up. A group of the girl's friends lounged beside the swimming pool passing a reefer around. Todd wanted to pass it on but felt awkward among the young people, he didn't want them to think he was old and past it. The drag on the cigarette was deep, smoke entered his lungs and he began to relax. *Maybe it was a good idea,* he thought at the time. Freya wrapped herself around him and he stroked her hair. She was a sweet little thing.

When he woke in the morning, his head ached and his mouth felt dry. Todd rolled over to realise he was in bed beside a naked Freya. He moaned, crawled out and pulled on his clothes. He shouldn't be driving, but he picked up his keys and went back to his campsite.

After downing a strong cup of coffee, he sat with his head in his hands and berated himself. He felt foolish and dirty. *What do I think I'm doing? I can't even remember what happened. I'm such an idiot. Here it is Easter Sunday, and what have I been up to?* Guilt and shame enveloped him. He vowed he had to get his act together, he'd had enough already of his immature behaviour.

"I'm sure I had it in here," he rummaged through the stuff in the glove box. "Ah, there it is." Todd pulled out a small blue New Testament that he'd shoved in there years ago.

He found a sheltered spot in the sand dunes and opened the Bible. In Matthew 26 he began to read the Easter story, the last supper and about the Garden of Gethsemane and Judas' betrayal. That's just what he felt - he'd betrayed Jesus, and he'd denied him like Peter did before the crucifixion. All that Jesus did on the cross for his sin burdened his soul.

He felt dark, tears streamed down his face. His soul was lost, and he knew the truth because he'd been taught it from when he was a little boy. He'd ignored it but now his filthy heart was exposed, and he couldn't keep going without confessing all he'd done before a holy God. There were things he wished he hadn't done, but couldn't undo now. He prayed and poured out his darkness before the Lord until light filled his soul instead. He was made clean, forgiven and free. Todd wanted to dance, to run and jump for joy.

Why had he waited so long? He couldn't explain it, but he knew he'd changed inside and could feel it. He was bought with a price, the cost of Jesus' life for his. Wow! His weekend had taken a turn, a good one, and he couldn't wait to tell his parents. He knew God had answered their prayers, and he understood why it was important to them. *Thank you, Lord.* His life would never be the same again.

Courtney's Easter weekend had been like no other she'd experienced before. Millie had taken her to church on Friday and Sunday, twice in three days. It was a lovely church building, and the people were friendly and made her feel welcome. The nave was filled with beautiful flower arrangements. Families filled the pews on Easter Sunday.

The Reverend spoke about Jesus' death and resurrection, and it was more real than she'd ever known. While she was growing up it was about a hot cross bun on Friday and an Easter egg on Sunday, the only special things they got at the Home other than a small gift at Christmas. There were a lot of things to think about and absorb. Still more confusion to clutter her mind, along with the verses she'd read in the Bible.

Millie had asked her if she wanted to join the Ladies' Bible Study group with some of her friends. Courtney wasn't sure that's what she wanted to do but a nagging desire to have some questions answered compelled her to say she would go. Now she felt nervous thinking about it. *Would Millie understand if I change my mind? No, I can't let her down, not after all she's done for me, that wouldn't be fair.*

Late on Tuesday afternoon, a telegram was delivered to her door. It read: Bank Manager found loophole STOP Need time STOP Wired money to post office STOP Letter in mail STOP Jacob Hoyle. Courtney held the bit of paper in her hand and read it several times. It was not going to be an easy issue to fix after all. She trusted the lawyer but wondered what was going to happen if it went on for a long time.

Bible study was held on Wednesday in the church building at 10 o'clock. Courtney was only just on time and shyly poked her head around the door. Millie saw her and waved her into the foyer. Helen York and Maureen, whom she already knew, were there. Millie introduced her to Mavis, Trudy and Ethel. Mavis took her by the arm to show her the building.

"I know you've been to church before but you haven't had a chance to have a good look around." Mavis explained about the nameplates on the ends of the pews. Ethel joined them and expounded a discourse on the history of the church.[2]

Millie summoned the women into the church hall. Courtney noticed and admired the old pressed tin ceiling when she walked in. The ladies sat around a table with their Bibles and study books open. The Reverend's wife opened the meeting in prayer. They took turns reading verses out loud. These women were kind, and made Courtney feel comfortable enough to ask a few questions. It was an interesting discussion, and some of the ladies shared from their own experiences.

One thing that seemed to keep coming up was they trusted God to provide for their needs in every circumstance. That was 'faith', they said. It was a concept she'd never explored before. After a time of earnest prayer they shared a quick morning tea and parted company.

She didn't say much to Millie afterwards and told her she had to go to the post office. After signing for the $100 cash and walking home, she checked the letterbox. An official envelope postmarked 'Sydney, NSW' was waiting for her. Courtney sighed. She didn't want to find out what was in the letter but had no choice except to see what Jacob Hoyle had to say.

The foolscap sheet of paper with an embossed letterhead bore its news, and Courtney sat with her elbows on the table and her head resting in her hands. Courtney's mind reeled at the memory of the prayer time earlier in the day. It was deep, and real as if they were talking to a friend but with awesome respect. It was like God knew and understood them. How she longed for a relationship like that.

---

2 All Saints Anglican Church

"Oh God, I need your help. I don't know how this is going to turn out but this problem needs to be solved. I'm mad with the bank manager and I don't like him. How can he be so cruel to tie up my inheritance like this? Please show me what to do."

The young woman prayed aloud, and even though it sounded strange to her own ears, a sense of peace surrounded her. She had to trust God, and have faith in Him to answer her prayer.

CHAPTER 6

A sarcastic voice right behind Courtney stopped her in her tracks as she walked down the Co-op grocery aisle. "I hope you've got enough money to pay for that?" She turned to face Gordon Prescott looking down his long sharp nose at her.

"I'll thank you to mind your own business," was her curt reply.

"But you are my business, aren't you, Missy?" he snorted and strode out of the shop.

Courtney quickly shoved the rest of the items she needed into her hand-held basket and approached the counter. The woman at the checkout looked like she was about to spit venom.

"Don't worry about him, and if you need credit, I'm sure we can arrange an approved account for you. Horrid man."

Courtney was relieved at the comment. She'd thought she would be the one accosted after the public display she had been subjected to by the bank manager. A headache behind her eyes began to build on the walk home, and she needed a drink of water and a Panadol.

There was a slip of paper under the back door in the kitchen. Courtney noticed it when she put the paper bags of shopping on the table. It was a note from Millie.

Dear Courtney,
You have a message from Jacob Hoyle to ring him,
reverse charges, to discuss the issues with the bank.
Come and make the call from my place when you're
ready. I'll be home all day today.
Love, Millie

Unsure of what to expect, Courtney delayed the telephone call until she remembered that the eastern states were ahead of WA by two hours. She needed to ring before the close of business. *"Nothing for it, but to go and do it, Courtney,"* she mentored herself. Millie assured her it was all right to use her phone and explained how to make a reverse charge phone call.

"I'll go and sit on the verandah and give you some privacy," Millie made to go outside.

"No, Millie. Stay, please. I might need your advice."

Millie sat at the kitchen table and waited.

"Hello, Mr Hoyle. It's Courtney Lancaster here."

Jacob responded, and the room was quiet while the young woman listened to the lawyer.

"Oh, no. I don't understand."

"But how would he know that?"

The one-sided conversation continued, Millie was concerned for her young friend.

"All right, I can't do anything else about it."

"Yes, I'm grateful for that. Thank you."

Courtney put the receiver back and sat down.

"He's doing all he can, Millie, but somehow Gordon Prescott has become aware of the discrepancy of my name from when I was in the Home."

"Discrepancy?" Millie looked confused.

"Yes, the Matron consistently used 'Lancashire' as my surname instead of Lancaster even though I kept telling her it was wrong. I was reprimanded for being rude and interrupting an adult, then told to be quiet because I was a child. Eventually, I gave up trying to right the wrong."

"What's the problem with the bank then?"

"The manager has put a legal query over my identity which stops any more payments from Uncle Geoff's account. Apparently, he has a right to do that until the courts determine I am the person that I say I am. I don't understand how he could know about the name issue, though. Mr Hoyle said it could be tied up in a court case for a long time. The lawyers' company has decided to send me money through the post office once a fortnight, but it's only a small amount to get me by."

After dinner, while Courtney was doing the dishes, she saw the business card propped up on the mantelpiece. It gave her an idea, maybe Mr Crawford could employ her. She didn't have a car and couldn't travel to Frankland every day, but there might be a bus and a room to stay in out there.

She would ring him tomorrow. Not having her own phone was a nuisance, and she had been going to get one put in but wouldn't be able to now without enough money to pay for it. Fortunately, Millie didn't mind if she used her telephone, and she could leave some coins to pay for the calls.

Keith Crawford was pleased with himself. Courtney Lancaster had rung him looking for his help, and he was happy to offer it. It was timely, too. He was going to visit her when he was in Mt Barker on Thursday.

The Bible study ladies prayed with their new recruit about the problems she was facing. She appreciated the advice they gave after Millie suggested she share her story with them. No-one in the group knew Mr Crawford, but one woman who came from Rocky Gully had heard of someone who'd come to live in the area from Perth a little while ago. She thought it might be the same person. Courtney felt comfort with the care and concern they gave. Tomorrow would prove to be either a resolution or a dead-end idea.

The bell on the front door rang. Courtney had dressed neatly in a smart grey skirt with a button-through pink floral shirt and wore white sandals to complete the outfit. Her makeup was immaculate, and she'd tied her hair back with a ribbon to match her top. Nervous anticipation of the encounter came to the fore as she walked up the passage.

"Hello, Mr Crawford. Please, come in."

Courtney felt strange inviting a man she didn't know into the house. She was glad Millie was coming over in half an hour to make sure everything was all right.

"Thank you." He was polite.

She noticed his brown hair and sideburns had a few strands of grey, and warm brown eyes sat under neat eyebrows on his tanned face.

"Um, take a seat."

He sat in the old armchair facing the fireplace in the lounge room. She sat opposite on the couch by herself.

"This is a bit awkward, sorry. I really need to find a job, and when I saw your business card that you'd given me a few weeks ago, I thought of your offer to help out."

"It would be my pleasure. How do you think I might be able to do that?" the man asked.

"Well, I'm happy to work in the vineyard, or maybe you need help with some office duties. I'd do anything you ask, I need an income and I need it soon."

"Okay. How would you feel about being a hostess for me?"

Courtney started. In Sydney 'a hostess' was often used as a polite term for prostitution at dance clubs. That was not the type of work she wanted. She let out a nervous breath.

"What do you mean by that?"

"I have a business arrangement with a winemaker and marketing manager for the winery. They need to come from Perth for three nights a week, Thursday through to Sunday morning for six months. I can't have them at the property. They've said they don't want to stay at the hotel because Friday and Saturday nights are usually noisy. And there is only a shared bathroom." He paused to give her time to take in the details.

"What do you propose?" Courtney wasn't sure what he was getting at.

"Could you accommodate them here at your house? They would only be here for breakfast and dinner and out at the vineyard all day. You would hardly even see them."

"But I haven't got much room, and only one bathroom ... although, I could ... no, sorry I don't have any money to do that now."

"That's my point, I'm happy to lend you an interest-free loan to make the place suitable and pay you for their board. We won't worry about repayments until your issues with the bank are sorted out." She'd forgotten he was aware of her situation. "How would $35 per night sound?"

Courtney did a quick mental calculation. Times three nights, plus half the $100 a fortnight would make it $155 per week. Could she manage with the extra costs for that amount?

"I don't know. I might need to think about it, but it's a possibility."

The doorbell rang, and Courtney excused herself. She quickly ran the option by Millie at the door.

"What do you think?"

The older woman shrugged, unsure of the details.

"Let's ask some more questions."

Introductions were made, and an amicable conversation followed. Millie's probing revealed that the sum was $35 per person per night and they were a married couple so would only need one room. Courtney was stunned, $260 cash a week was more than she'd ever earned before. It would need to be ready for them after the long weekend in June, but it was a deal she could accept.

Discussion about how to go about making changes to the house ensued. Everyone was pleased with the outcome. Keith shook hands with Courtney, a heartfelt thank you left his lips and the gentleman headed for the door. The smiling ladies followed him out to the front verandah to say goodbye.

"Thanks again," Keith re-iterated his pleasure at their arrangement. Then he decided to give Courtney a hug. Todd was working over the road and witnessed the whole scene. He was cross and felt a jealous pang shoot through him. He went over after the man drove off.

"What's with that bloke? Isn't he the stalker? And he's old enough to be your father." Todd was a bit short in his attitude.

"No, he's not a stalker. He's just a very nice man."

"Hmph, a nice man? How do you know that?"

"Because he just came to my rescue ... and created some more work for you. If you want it."

They explained the plan, and then explored how the sleep-out could be extended, adding a bathroom and the permissions that would be needed from the Council. Todd was excited to do the project even if it would be pressured for time.

"Courtney, I'm sorry about earlier. You know, when I arrived."

Todd's remorse was genuine. She hadn't noticed his abruptness earlier and was surprised at his apology.

"You're different. I could sense that while we were talking out the back."

"Yep, I've become a bona fide Christian."

He beamed at his announcement.

"When did that happen?"

"Easter, over at Margaret River. I'll tell you about it one day."

He bounced down the path and jumped in his ute.

Millie stood there, silent, watching him go with tears glistening in her eyes.

"Well, well. Thank you, Lord. See Courtney, God does answer prayer."

"Oh, no!"

"What is it?"

Millie didn't understand why she would say that.

"I don't know how to cook, and I have to give them breakfast and dinner. What have I done? I didn't think about that when I was calculating the money, did I?"

"That's easily fixed. I'll teach you, starting today. You can come and help me make a meatloaf for dinner with mashed potatoes, steamed carrots and runner beans. Meat and three veg, a well-balanced diet. What have you been eating if you don't know how to cook?"

"I have tinned spaghetti or baked beans on toast and I can make a sandwich or a can of soup. I eat fruit and veggies, too."

"Any wonder you are stick thin, my girl."

Courtney leaned over and hugged her neighbour, thankful for the help she was going to get in the coming days. Although, if she knew how difficult it would be she might not have been so anxious to get those cooking lessons started.

"No. Not like that, you need to be careful. Just tap the egg gently and then break it open. Tip the yolk into the other half of the shell and let the egg white slide off into the bowl. Don't rush it or the yellow will split and spoil the white."

Courtney followed the instructions again, and was pleased when it worked this time. Finally, she managed to separate six eggs. Two other eggs sat in a separate bowl, broken. Millie claimed she would make an omelette with them.

"That's it, well done."

The egg whites were beaten until soft peaks formed, caster sugar was added and beaten until it dissolved and the glossy thick mixture stiffened. Millie showed her how to whisk in the cornflour, vinegar and vanilla until they were just combined. The student placed blobs of meringue within the circle marked out on the aluminium foil and built up the pavlova ready to go in the oven. It wasn't perfect but Millie was pleased with her efforts. One and a half hours later they turned off the heat and left the pavlova in the oven while it cooled.

"That is the quintessential Australian dessert, Courtney. Not everyone can master it, but you've made a good job of it today. It's all practice, that's what it is. The more often you do it the better you'll get."

Courtney quite liked cooking, once she got over the frustration of understanding the processes and method instructions in a recipe. She'd learnt not to 'adjust' the quantities herself when the beef curry burnt her mouth because she thought it needed a bit more spice.

She'd managed to get spaghetti Bolognese, meatloaf with vegetables and a homemade chicken soup added to her cooking repertoire. Those things Courtney could make confidently. That was after burning the potatoes to a charred black mess because she hadn't put enough water in the saucepan. It took half an hour to scrub the pot clean and she'd had to start again. Learning when pasta was cooked 'al dente' was tricky but if she checked it regularly she managed to avoid overcooking it to a gluggy mess.

The young woman realised how much she'd missed by living in an institution instead of a family environment. Millie was an expert cook, and was patient with her while she struggled to cut up an onion, learned how to boil rice and make a custard without lumps. Eating the delicious results was the best part of the whole exercise. Then she had to clean up her mess, do the dishes and wipe down the stove and benches. Sometimes she spilled food on the floor and had to mop as well. Both women had a stash of meals in their freezers from the leftovers. It was exhausting and Courtney would fall into bed and sleep soundly every night.

CHAPTER 7

The plans were drawn up and submitted to the Shire Council for approval. Courtney was excited by the whole venture. Todd was pleased with the final sketches, but it had been a challenge to make it all work. He made arrangements with Keith Crawford for an account at Mt Barker Hardware Store for the general items he would need. Payment of invoices from Albany timber and window suppliers were going to be sent direct to Keith. Todd had to admit he was 'a nice man'. They'd met several times to discuss the choice of products and enjoyed each other's company.

Monday, May 5th, 1980 was commencement day of the project. The building licence had been granted, and there wasn't time to waste. Todd was out there digging footings for the posts to hold the bearers and joists for the new floor. He set the four by four inch jarrah stumps into concrete, then propped and plumbed them straight. Jarrah tongue and groove floorboards were on order and would be delivered in a week.

In the meantime, Todd removed the glass louvres from the windows and prised the frames off the existing enclosed verandah. The glass was brittle, and some of it broke. The demolition of the wall panelling went into the trailer next, and lino was stripped off the floor. It was all taken to the local rubbish dump. Todd liked a tidy site, a legacy of the builder he'd worked for previously.

Progress went smoothly on the job. Keith called in on Mondays to check out the work while he was in Mt Barker. Courtney would make lunch for the men and they'd discuss any issues that had come up during the week. One Monday lunchtime the doorbell rang, and when Courtney opened the door Gordon Prescott was standing on the top step.

"What do you want?" Courtney had difficulty in being civil to this impudent man.

"I want to know how you're paying for that building going on out the back?"

"Quite frankly, it's none of your business."

"Just who do you think you are, Missy?" The snide comment rolled off his tongue easily.

Keith and Todd had heard the conversation, and both got up from the table at the same time and exited the room.

"Courtney, if it's all right with you I'll handle this," Keith uttered quietly under his breath. She nodded and was happy for him to take control of the situation. Todd stood beside her and Keith stepped out onto the front verandah. The bank manager was surprised by his presence.

"Sir, I'm asking you to leave. Now, please." Keith directed his instruction to Gordon Prescott while looking straight at him.

"What have you got to do ... oh, so you're the one behind all this," he waved his hand around pointing at the rear of the house.

"Miss Lancaster was right in telling you that it's none of your business."

"I suppose you're the one paying the bills. Who are you borrowing the money from? I know it's not my bank," Prescott pushed a little further.

"I don't need to borrow the money from you or anyone else," Keith stated.

A surprised glance passed between Todd and Courtney.

"What are you?" he scoffed. "A millionaire? What's in it for you?" Prescott snorted his disgusting laugh at the composed man before him.

"Even if I am, it's none of your concern. I'm asking you politely to leave, or I will ring the police. Don't come anywhere near Miss Lancaster or her property again. Otherwise, legal action will be taken against you for harassment. Do you understand?" Keith was becoming annoyed.

"Yeah, I get it. You don't need to be like that. I'm just trying to do my job." Gordon Prescott turned and left, seething with frustration.

"You sure told him," Courtney said brightly.

"Only a threat, his kind like to throw their assumed power around when they think they can get away with it. I don't expect he'll be around again, but if he does show up, you must let me know Courtney. I'm glad you're here every day Todd, I don't trust that man one bit."

They resumed the meal they'd started but everyone had lost their appetite. Keith left a little while later to finish his business in town.

"Do you think Keith is a millionaire?" Todd queried. He wanted to know what Courtney thought.

"Maybe he is. He didn't deny it. Wouldn't that be amazing? Maybe he's wealthy but wanted the horrible man to think he was richer than he is."

"I reckon he is a millionaire, it's not like Keith to be deceitful."

Todd went back to the building site to finish the afternoon work he'd planned. Thoughts of the man they were involved with churned around in his head for the rest of the day. *I wonder who he is?*

They drove past the airport on their way to Albany. Courtney reminisced about arriving on the plane.

"Haven't you been into town before?" Todd wanted to know.

"No, this is my first time."

"Sorry, I didn't realise. I could've taken you if you'd wanted to go."

"I hadn't thought about it, but I'm glad I've come with you today."

"Because of the pact we made that we are just friends?"

"Especially because of that," Courtney smiled at him.

Todd took her for a drive past the Town Hall, and along Stirling Terrace where he pointed out the Old Post Office. There was a restaurant in the building poignantly called 'The Penny Post.' She went shopping in the main street and admired the view of the harbour. The cold wind whipped up York Street and chilled her to the bone making her wish she'd worn a jacket. She'd remember for next time.

They drove to Mt Clarence and saw the steps that ascended to the Desert Mounted Corps Memorial. There wasn't time to go and have a look, but they could plan to do it another day. The view from Marine Drive across King George Sound was stunning. Middleton Beach curled around in a crescent of white beach sand lined with green grass and tall Norfolk pines. Courtney didn't realise how much bigger Albany was compared to Mt Barker, she'd expected it to be another small town.

"Does York Street have any connection to your family?" Courtney wanted to know.

"Never thought about it before, I guess I should ask my Dad." He commented as they drove home.

"Can you bring something to break the lock on the old shed tomorrow?" Courtney asked when Todd dropped her off. She hadn't found a key anywhere to unlock it. He agreed he could.

Armed with bolt cutters the pair stood at the door, and jiggled the rigid lock on the shed. Snap went the brass, and it cut clean through. Todd pulled on the stiff door and had it partly open when Courtney grabbed his arm and jumped up and down.

"The trunk, the trunk's in there," she was excited and behaved like a child finding a treasure chest. "Let me in I want to see what's in it."

"Hang on a minute, I've got a bug bomb to set off first."

She hadn't noticed the mass of spider webs across the whole room.

"There'll be red-backs and whitetails in there."

"Can't we just get a broom and sweep them aside?"

"No, you can't risk being bitten. You'll have to wait until tomorrow." Todd said gently.

"Aw, that's cruel, I don't want to wait. What time can we come in the morning?"

Todd smiled at her disappointment and enthusiasm expressed in the same breath.

"First thing, okay?"

She pouted, but nodded in response.

Courtney waited on the back steps with the odd shaped key for the trunk in one hand and a broom in the other. She greeted Todd with a cheeky grin when he arrived. He laughed, he should have known what to expect.

"All right, let's go and have a look."

The cobwebs and dust were thick but swept aside easily. Courtney started sneezing, and her hand shook as she wiped the lock clean and put the key in the trunk. It turned without any effort. The young woman looked up at Todd.

"Here goes," and she lifted the lid. The folded brown paper on top of the contents had 'For Courtney' written on it. Underneath was a stack of Uncle Geoff's diaries, a photo album and a large box tied up with string. She beamed a smile of satisfaction, she had found treasure. More than she realised at the time.

The trunk sat on the kitchen floor, abandoned, its contents piled on the laminex table. It was the photo album that intrigued Courtney the most. A large black and white photo of a bride and groom on the steps in front of a church was on the first page. When she looked closely, she realised it was her parents. She turned the page and gasped. There were photos of a baby in a bassinet, sitting up on a blanket and in a bathtub of bubbles. It was her! *Me, photos of me.* She couldn't believe it.

The pages bore pictures of herself with her Mum and Dad at the beach, in the park, at the zoo and her Grade One school photo. She looked through the album again, and again. It took her breath away to realise this was her history. It was a part of her life she couldn't remember, and here it was revealed where she had never expected to find it.

The back door creaked and interrupted her intense concentration. Todd came into the laundry to wash his hands before lunch. *Had that much time gone by?* She hadn't realised.

"Look, Todd. Come and see this, it's me when I was a baby with my parents."

He relished her excitement of the discovery. They flipped through the diaries quickly and Courtney promised she would read every one of them. The box would have to wait until after they'd eaten. They sat on the front verandah to have their sandwich, and when they finished took the lunch dishes in and put them on the sink.

"Do you want me to stay while you open this?" Todd asked her. "Otherwise, I'll go back to work."

"Stay, please."

The string was removed, the tape broken and they peered into the box to discover a teddy, a doll's house and a package of baby clothes. Tears ran down Courtney's face, toys and clothes, these things had belonged to her.

"I wonder how Uncle Geoff ended up with them?" she asked Todd while he handed her another brown paper package.

"The music box!" It was a beautiful glossy black lacquer with red and gold Chinese etchings over it. "I have the key," Courtney ran to her room and got the tiny key.

They unlocked the box and lifted the lid. A ballerina spun around to the music, fascinating them both. A little drawer on one side was pulled out, and inside were two wedding rings and an engagement ring. Her parents' initials were engraved inside the 18 carat gold bands with 'M and C forever'.

"Michael and Claire forever," she whispered.

Courtney sobbed in Todd's arms.

"Geoffrey must have been given these things after they passed away."

Why did they have to die? All I ever wanted was to know my parents. God, it's not fair. Please help me to understand why it happened, she prayed.

Todd popped into the house before he left for the night. He could hear the music box playing in the lounge room. Courtney sat there with the photo album open on her lap and was mesmerised by the pirouetting ballerina.

"Shall I get Millie to come over?" he asked quietly.

She nodded, and he said goodbye.

Millie took a plate of dinner for Courtney and encouraged her to eat it. They'd looked at the photos and cried together. Later Millie tucked Courtney into bed and closed the lid on the music box.

"Go to sleep sweetheart, you're exhausted after all that emotional turmoil. I'll stay with you for a little while."

The young woman didn't take long to succumb to the rest her body needed.

Courtney woke at about four o'clock in the morning and couldn't go back to sleep. She sat up in bed with the lamp on after she'd picked up one of Uncle Geoff's diaries to read. It was the one off the top of the heap and was a record of the jobs he'd worked on as an engineer with the Main Roads Department. An hour later she was sound asleep again and didn't wake until she heard a loud truck engine outside her bedroom window.

The concrete had been ordered for the bathroom floor, and was being poured. She was missing the action. Courtney got dressed, brushed her hair and cleaned her teeth quickly before she went outside to watch what they were doing. Todd had the form-work set up, and the concrete was being dumped from the wheelbarrow onto the plastic lining and steel mesh. A labourer shovelled in the wet concrete to level it off, and Todd followed along with a screed to compress it and smooth the surface. After the truck left they drank ice-cold lemon barley cordial and chatted.

"How are you feeling today?" Todd wiped the sweat off his face and the back of his neck with an old towel.

"Still a bit sad, but I slept okay. Millie's so lovely; she took care of me last night. I did wake up in the early hours of the morning though, so I got a diary to read. You'd be interested in it, I think."

"Me?" he asked, curious. "Why?"

"There are records about bridges Uncle Geoff helped build in Perth years ago."

"Do you know which ones they were?"

"A causeway it was called, over the Swan River, and I can't remember what the other one was."

"Can you get it? You're right, I am interested."

While Todd waited for the concrete to set, he poured over the details and sketches of the Causeway and the Narrows Bridge. Geoffrey had been an engineer with the government department while they were under construction. He'd written meticulous notes, and Todd found it fascinating. Courtney told him they'd bored her back to sleep. The building inspector came in the afternoon. He was impressed with the quality of the work and ticked off several requirements that had been met on his list.

There were only two weeks left before the end of May. The framework had to be lined, the corrugated iron needed to be put on the roof timbers and then plumbing and electrical wiring could be installed. It was good progress, and Todd hoped the fine weather would hold out. It was common to get heavy showers of rain at this time of the year, and he didn't need that kind of interruption.

CHAPTER 8

It did rain. A light shower developed into a pouring torrent. The building site was a quagmire, and Todd needed to cover part of the new area to keep working. He balanced on a slippery ladder while he tied a tarpaulin across the bathroom rafters. Courtney was worried while she watched him from inside the back door. It was dangerous, and she thought he should wait until it cleared up. It wasn't worth the risk of falling and breaking an arm or leg because that would be an even worse delay.

In the late afternoon a shaft of sunlight peeked between the clouds with the promise of a clearing sky. Fortunately, the rain didn't persist overnight. It was a stunning Autumn day when Todd got to work, and although everything was wet, it didn't hold him up.

On Monday, one week before the building deadline, Keith Crawford turned up for his usual visit. He was impressed with how much had been achieved in such a short time. The men discussed final fit-out and electrical connection details and asked Courtney about curtains and blinds for the windows. At the lunch table Keith seemed unusually quiet.

"Are you all right?" Courtney couldn't resist the temptation to enquire.

"Yes. I want you to know how much I appreciate what you've both done for me."

The puzzled pair looked at one another.

"Done for you? It's more like what you've done for me," Courtney said.

"And me," Todd added. I've enjoyed the challenge of this job. It's been satisfying and a generous boost to my income."

"Just the same, it's been important that the addition was ready to go on time. Thank you."

That was another cryptic statement from Keith that they didn't quite understand. Courtney cleared the table while they discussed re-sealing the driveway. It hadn't mattered to Courtney because she didn't have a car, but the guests needed a decent parking space.

A few days later they went into Albany to buy furniture and linen. The bed was set up by Todd, and Courtney made the bed with crisp white sheets and pillowslips. She had plenty of practice in the past, to specific standards too. Matron was fastidious about making the bed properly, and it had to be done over and over if it wasn't good enough. Courtney had made many beds for the younger girls in her dormitory to protect them from being punished. It was the least she could do, and they were always thankful. It was the only time she'd felt of any worth in the place.

Millie admired the lovely bedroom with its pastel blue walls and white furniture. The floral curtains at the large window were a blue and white chintz with sheer terylene curtains for privacy. A plain royal blue Velour quilt was on the bed. Todd had sealed the jarrah floorboards and the warmth of the timber highlighted the colours.

The bathroom boasted light blue mosaic tiles on the floor with blue and white patterned tiles on the walls.

Courtney had put dark blue towels with white hand towels on the rails ready for use. Millie praised the young people for the wonderful job they'd done. The gift of a bunch of flowers from her garden sat in a vase on the chest of drawers. Courtney was excited about the guests coming to stay, although she had to push away an uneasy niggle at the back of her mind.

A black Mercedes Benz sports car pulled up on the newly sealed tarmac, Keith had already parked his car across the road and rushed over to Courtney. She was dressed in her best clothes ready to greet the guests. Keith stood beside her and smiled, but he was sweating.

A jolly man alighted from the expensive vehicle and went around to the passenger's side to open the door for his wife. A blonde woman exited the car gracefully. She was dressed in designer label clothes and wore stiletto heels. She left her sunglasses on. Keith made the introductions.

"Jerry and Kate, this is Courtney. This is where you'll be staying."

"Courtney, this is Jerry Keller and Kate Smythe."

Courtney smiled and put her hand out which Jerry grabbed hold of and warmly shook. Kate just nodded.

"It's nice to meet you, please come in and have some refreshments."

The table was laid out with a freshly ironed tablecloth, four plates and embroidered napkins; and a bowl of pink camellias sat in the centre. A dish with Anzac biscuits, a milk jug and the sugar were covered with a sheer throw. The cups and saucers were on the kitchen bench ready to make a cup of tea or coffee, or she could offer lemon barley cordial in a tall chilled glass. Millie had coached her with the finer points of presentation, and Courtney thought it all looked lovely. Keith squeezed her arm and smiled, he was impressed with her efforts.

Jerry pulled the laminex chair out for Kate and flashed her a warning look. *"Don't!"* his eyes said. Courtney didn't notice. The kettle had boiled, and she accidentally spilled hot water on her hand when filling the teapot. She didn't want to get flustered but she couldn't help it. Pretending to wash her hands she turned the cold water tap on and shoved her hand under it. It still burned. The tea was poured and she offered the biscuit plate around. Keith and Jerry took one each, but Kate refused with a wave of her hand.

"This is delicious, did you make them?" Jerry asked as he took another one for himself.

"Yes," Courtney replied quietly, with hands folded in her lap.

She became agitated, and Keith sensed her nervousness. He offered to show the guests to their room and bring in their luggage.

A huge sigh escaped from Courtney's lips when they all left the room. *Can I do this?*

Keith came back into the kitchen.

"I thought you said they were married?"

"They are," he looked puzzled.

"Oh, how come they've got different names then?"

"Some women keep their maiden name for business reasons." She raised an eyebrow at his comment. "You've done a great job,

Courtney, well done. They'll have breakfast at nine o'clock tomorrow before they come out to the vineyard."

"Not until nine? That's a bit late, isn't it?"

"You can have your breakfast whenever you're ready. They'll expect to eat theirs by themselves anyway. Good luck." He smiled and waved goodbye.

Great, now I have to face this alone.

Dinner was prepared but it was too early to get it ready. Courtney did the afternoon tea dishes and re-set the table for the evening meal, and then put a cold pack on her burned hand. The clock ticked and time seemed to go by slowly. She could hear mumbling from the new room on the other side of the kitchen.

Dinner was awkward. Kate had showered and changed into a pair of cream slacks with a pastel blue shirt and silk scarf. She'd taken her glasses off, and Courtney was stunned by the clear blue eyes that reflected a hard steel-like demeanour. Jerry was jovial and tried to make conversation, but it fell flat every time.

"Where are we supposed to spend the evening?" The curt request came from Kate, the first words she'd directed at her hostess.

Courtney was taken aback.

"Um, well you can use the lounge room. There is a black and white TV in there if you want to watch it, but the reception isn't very good. There's a radio and an old cassette player with some tapes on the coffee table." Kate shrugged her shoulders and sighed as she threw a quick glance at Jerry.

"We'll use it," she replied bluntly.

Courtney cleared up and went to her room with one of Uncle Geoff's diaries. She wasn't welcome to join them and didn't want to anyway.

"You don't have to be so rude, Kate, it's not that hard to make an effort to be polite," Jerry's voice could be heard across the passageway.

"Well, what do you expect? It's hardly five-star accommodation," Kate stated.

"Courtney is a charming young lady, and she's gone out of her way to put us up," Jerry defended. "It's only for a few days."

"Every week, for the next six months." Kate had her Vogue magazine open and flipped through the pages until she found something that interested her. They went to their room around 10.00pm, and Courtney tiptoed out to the kitchen for a cuppa and snack.

What am I doing? I don't have to sneak around in my own house.

Sunday couldn't come soon enough for Courtney, and at last, the guests finished their breakfast which they'd had earlier than on the other two days. Thank goodness, she was as eager for them to leave as Kate was to go back to the city. The couple left in their car and Courtney breathed a sigh of relief. She sat in her favourite chair on the front verandah with a nice hot cup of tea.

It was the bank manager's fault. If he hadn't frozen her account, she wouldn't have to put up with that woman, but she did have to and was determined to make the best of it. At least Jerry was friendly. Courtney decided she'd go to church with Millie.

"Turn to the book of Mark, chapter 12 and verses 30 and 31," the Reverend said after they'd sung some hymns. "We're going to look at loving God and loving others."

The message was clear, we are to love God with everything we are and have, and love our neighbour as ourselves. Courtney felt uncomfortable and talked to Millie on the way home. She told her about the situation with the guests.

"How am I supposed to love someone I don't even like? I don't want to love her, Millie."

"It's about loving with God's love, Courtney. Sometimes we can't love people because they simply do not endear themselves to us. However, God can give us his power to love them the same way he does, and if you trust God to show you how, you will be able to do it."

"It's not going to be easy," Courtney shook her head.

"No, but it's a good life lesson," Millie changed the subject, "Are you going to come to church with me again next week?"

"Yes, I think I'll need the encouragement after three days of Kate Smythe!"

Thank God for friends like Millie, and yes, even Todd.

CHAPTER 9

An argument erupted in the next room. Courtney stood at the kitchen sink washing the dishes after dinner was finished.

"I don't know why we had to come back here, Jerry." Kate's voice boomed.

"This is where we are staying, and there's no alternative, so just get used to it," Jerry yelled back at his wife.

"I don't see why we have to, there's room at the vineyard. Tell Keith we have to go there, you are being gutless."

"No, Kate. This was the deal and it's not going to change."

A crashing sound followed his statement.

"What was that?" Courtney whispered to herself. Something got broken, and she hoped it wasn't the old vase she'd found in the kitchen cupboard. The door opened and a red-faced Kate stood before her.

"Can you come and clean up the mess in here ... please?" she added reluctantly.

It was the vase, shattered on the timber floor with water and flowers strewn across it. Courtney held back tears while she collected the broken glass and mopped up the boards. Kate was an awful woman. *You'd better help me here, God, I want to scream at her. How dare she do this?*

No apology was offered, and Courtney bit her tongue and left the room. Jerry came out afterwards to speak to her.

"Look, I'm really sorry, I shouldn't have provoked her. I know she throws things when she gets mad. I'll replace it, and don't take any notice of what she said either. I'm grateful that we're here, really, I am." Jerry was shaken and embarrassed.

"Don't worry about it," she said, "the vase was an old one."

But it was my favourite, and it was Uncle Geoff's, she wanted to add but didn't. The house was quiet that evening and the lounge room was free. The weather had turned cold and the warmth from the open fireplace welcomed her in. Courtney enjoyed being on the couch with her feet tucked under her and a new diary to read. Before she opened it a thought occurred to her, it was something Kate had said earlier. *'There's room at the vineyard,'* strange ... if there was room out there, why did Keith want to build the extra room and have them stay here.

Courtney mulled that over for a while and could imagine why he wouldn't want to put up with Kate. Did he already know what she was like? If so, how come? And why would he inflict her upon someone else? Too many unanswered questions, and she couldn't ask him either. Keith hadn't been back into town to see her.

Todd was mowing the lawn across the road. Courtney went over and waved him down.

"Can you come over when you're finished here?" she yelled.

"Yeah," and then added, "What for? I did your lawns last week."

"Not about the lawns ...," she left the sentence in mid-air.

"Oh, okay. You better get a cold drink ready for me." He threw a smile at her and kept going. It wasn't long before he finished the job, loaded his gear and walked across the road.

"Here's your drink."

Courtney had been sitting on the verandah watching and waiting for him. She passed the tall glass over. He downed it in one swig.

"Ah, that was good." He refilled his glass from the frosty jug on the table and sipped it this time. "So what's this all about?"

"I need to debrief," she said.

"De-brief ... oh, you mean you need to talk?" He grinned at his play on her word usage.

"It's about my 'guests', and about Keith as well."

Todd changed his attitude immediately.

"What's going on?"

"It was something Kate said," she'd told him about the argument incident. "Keith's got room in his house at the vineyard where they could stay. I don't understand why they are coming here instead of going out there. I haven't seen Keith since the first day they arrived either."

"That's weird. What do you make of it?"

"I don't know, and I don't know what I should do or even if I should do anything at all."

"Why don't you invite Keith for dinner next Saturday? He'll come if you ask him, I'm sure of it. If you get the opportunity maybe you can have a quiet chat with him. You don't want to discuss this over the phone at Millie's, it's better to talk face to face."

"I like that idea, I'll do it." Sometimes Todd could be wise beyond his years. "Thanks," she felt relieved of the burden she'd been carrying.

"Any chance of some lunch?"

Courtney nodded.

"Sure, you deserve it."

The weather on Thursday was atrocious, the temperature had plummeted and the wind blew relentlessly. Showers of rain came and went throughout the day. Courtney was dreading Jerry and Kate coming, this was the third week they were due to arrive in the late afternoon.

The old Metters stove in the kitchen was lit and warmed the room. She had the fire going in the lounge room as well. About half an hour before the guests were due to arrive Courtney turned on the gas heater and put on the electric blankets in their bedroom. She'd made a shepherd's pie for dinner and chocolate self-saucing pudding for dessert. Kate never ate the sweets but Jerry loved it, his generous comments made her feel she'd achieved an element of success.

Kate walked into the house complaining about the weather, the long road trip and having to be at Courtney's house again. She refused to eat dinner and went straight to bed without even offering a courteous greeting. Jerry sat at the table with Courtney, and they had the opportunity to speak freely to each other. He asked about where she grew up and went to school. It surprised him to discover she was a ward-of-the-state and had come from Sydney recently. They chatted for a long while after they finished eating and Jerry helped her do the dishes.

Friday was much the same as the day before. The weather and Kate's mood were gloomy and irritable. Kate nibbled on a piece of toast and only drank a mouthful of her cup of tea before they set off for Frankland. Courtney busied herself with tidying up and decided what to make for dinner tomorrow night. She had a bit of shopping to do and popped in to see Millie.

Keith accepted the dinner invitation, and although somewhat reluctant, he couldn't refuse. A lasagne, tossed salad and garlic bread were on the menu with a pavlova to follow. The dessert was the first one Courtney had made all by herself, and she thought she'd done a pretty good job of it, too.

Six o'clock came and went. The lasagne was beginning to burn around the edges in the old oven. Six twenty, and still no Keith. Kate and Jerry were cosy in the lounge room with a glass of red wine while they waited. They weren't perturbed but Courtney was getting frantic, the meal would be ruined if he didn't hurry up. At six thirty, his car pulled into the driveway.

Kate must have heard the car arrive too, and she was in the kitchen straight away. Maybe she was hungry tonight, that wouldn't be surprising because she'd eaten little since arriving two days ago.

Keith walked in through the back door with a bashful look on his face and a bunch of shop-bought flowers.

"Oh, how sweet you are, flowers for me?" Kate was being sickly sweet and went to take the gift.

"No," he turned to Courtney. "These are for you. Sorry, I got held up and I feel awful making you wait." He handed the bouquet to her, and gave her a quick hug.

Kate fumed, and if she could have, she would've breathed fire on her hostess. She approached Keith but he quickly pulled out a chair at the end of the table and sat down.

"Right, let's eat. I'm starving, and you're probably more than ready to serve dinner, Courtney."

She nodded and pulled out a vase for the flowers, filled it with water and placed them in it. They could wait until later to be arranged. Jerry came in and greeted Keith warmly. He poured himself another glass of wine, and one for Keith.

"Would you like to try this Shiraz, Courtney?" he asked.

"I've never had any wine before."

The winemaker was surprised.

"Well, here you go," he poured a little in the glass for her. He went on to explain the aroma, the complexity of the flavours, the texture and other things she didn't understand.

Kate was very chatty at the table, and monopolised Keith, directing her conversation toward him. She was being so pleasant it was a surprise to Courtney. However, it was as if she wasn't even in the room, or Jerry for that matter. The pavlova was a triumph, Keith praised her for the delicious meal. Kate had even eaten dessert, and managed to compliment her. No sooner was the meal over when Keith said he had to go.

"What, already?" Kate took the words right out of Courtney's mouth. "No, darling, you must stay. We've got business to discuss."

"Not tonight, Kate, we'll talk about it next week."

Keith shook hands with Jerry, and hugged Courtney. He collected the dish with the leftovers he was taking for his lunch the next day and exited the room before Kate could reach him. And he was gone, and so was the nice lady who'd been in the room before.

"Well, you little tart, how dare you get in the way like that." She ripped into the younger woman.

"What? What do you mean?" Courtney couldn't believe what she was hearing.

"You know very well, what hold have you got on him?"

"Kate, that will be enough of that," Jerry said gruffly. "We'll say goodnight now Courtney, and thanks again for a lovely meal." He pushed his wife's back firmly in the direction of their room.

Astounded by the accusation, Courtney shook all over. *Does she think I'm having an affair with Keith?* Hardly, he was handsome and kind, and suave she supposed but was twice her age. Then she could see it clearly, it was Kate who was infatuated by him. Now it all made sense, no wonder Keith didn't want her out at his place in Frankland. Even Mt Barker was only just far enough away from him after having had to spend all day with her. *I wonder what the connection is?* She realised that Jerry was well aware of his wife's bad behaviour. That's why he insisted they stay here, even though Kate didn't want to.

The couple left before breakfast. Jerry had popped into the kitchen while Courtney was eating her toast and let her know they were leaving straight away. Relief washed over her, not in the least bit sorry that she didn't have to face that woman again this weekend. Five more months of this seemed like an eternity before it would be over.

Courtney opened the door to the guest room and was bowled over with the heat that rushed at her. The gas heater must have been left on since Thursday, and the electric blankets were still turned on as well. She stripped the bed and opened up the room to air it before she got ready to go to church. The Reverend would probably have another appropriate sermon to preach that she needed to hear. At least that would be a highlight after the weekend she'd just endured.

Tuesday was cooking lesson day, and Courtney stood beside Millie at the kitchen bench and followed her instructions. They only got together once a week since the intense sessions they'd had every day for a month. Scones were one of the recipes she couldn't master. The first batch weeks ago were so hard they could have bounced off the floor. Other batches were doughy or didn't rise very much.

"If these don't work this time, Millie, I'm going to give up."

"I suppose that's fair enough. There are some cooks who make different recipes better than others."

Millie didn't push the issue because it irked her to throw ingredients out, even if it was mainly flour and butter.

"You know, Millie, I find myself praying every now and then. Does that mean I believe in God?"

The older woman found herself smiling, she liked this kind of conversation.

"Well, you must do or you wouldn't bother, would you?"

"But I haven't had a dramatic experience, you know, like Todd. He told me about the day at the beach when he broke down before God. It was a passionate prayer, not like mine. They are more like questions."

"The Bible says – 'you will call on me and come and pray to me, and I will listen to you. You will seek me and find me when you seek me with all your heart.' I think that's what you're doing. Seeking God."

Courtney was dumbstruck.

"Are you all right? What have I said?"

"They're the words in Jeremiah, it's the other part of the verses about the future, plans and prospering."

Surprise lit Millie's face.

"How do you know about that?"

"I read it in Uncle Geoff's Bible. It was one of the verses in the birthday cards."

Millie was impressed, and encouraged Courtney to continue her search to know God.

CHAPTER 10

T he clock seemed to tick by slowly, waiting to announce its dreadful time bomb. Kate Smythe would be back in about two hours and thirty five minutes by Courtney's estimation. They arrived pretty much at the same time every week. How she feared the inevitable tongue lashing she knew would be forthcoming. *Brace yourself, Courtney,* she mentally admonished.

Right on time, Jerry bounced out of the car and ran up the steps. He was out of breath when he knocked on the door and poked his head into the kitchen.

"Hi, Courtney, will it be all right if I stay here by myself this weekend?"

Confusion clouded her eyes.

"Kate's in Melbourne on business. I'm concerned you might not want a man staying under your roof without someone else in the house. I could go to the Pub down the road if you prefer."

Relief washed over the young woman.

"That's okay, Jerry. You're welcome to stay here."

She knew he was trustworthy and didn't question her safety. All the anxiety she'd experienced earlier drained away.

The pair shared a convivial dinner together talking about a myriad of topics. Courtney decided to brave the subject of the missing wife.

"Jerry, I'd like to understand what it is that upsets Kate. I know she doesn't like coming here."

"It's got nothing to do with you, dear girl. Kate has issues, as you are well aware of from the short time we've been in your home. I appreciate your hospitality and apologise for Kate's lack of courtesy. It's good to have this time to chat freely."

"I don't want to pry into your private life, Jerry."

"No, I'm aware of that. Keith and I go back a long way and there's a lot of water under the bridge, so to speak. We grew up in the same suburb in Perth and were school buddies from Grade One right through to University. Kate and Keith dated for a short time but Keith confided in me that he wasn't as serious about their relationship as she was. I helped to break up the romance, but in the process, I fell in love with Kate myself.

We had an on-again, off-again relationship for several years until I decided it was time to commit permanently and asked Kate to marry me. I was elated when she accepted, and our love grew much deeper, but we weren't able to have children and Kate blames me. We've never had any tests done to prove the point, but it doesn't matter. Most of the time we are content together, and we have a happy life. Where Keith is concerned, though, she continues to hold that flicker of a flame which messes her up whenever he's around."

"You don't have to tell me all of this, Jerry."

"No, but I'd like you to understand her a bit better."

"It must have been disappointing for her not to be able to fall pregnant."

"Yes, it was. We've had counselling and therapy to overcome all of that. Keith and I catch up with each other occasionally by ourselves in a restaurant or bar somewhere in the city. That overcomes putting up with the unsettled feelings Kate has wondering if things might've been different with Keith."

"You're a patient man."

"Mostly, but sometimes I get a bit short with my wife, and I usually pay a price for it. It doesn't change the fact that I love Kate as much now as I ever did. We'll get through this once we've finished our work here."

"I wonder why Keith would ask you to come when he's aware of the circumstances."

"That's because he knows we are the best at what we do. I can tweak his wine harvest to make a unique palate for his wines and Kate is a leader in the Australian marketing business. She's in Melbourne right now working on a new label for Crawford Estate Winery with the top graphic designer in the field."

"I guess you put up with the awkward moments for the best results then."

"You're right. Keith always goes in headlong when he takes on a new venture, and it will be a raging success. I can assure you of that, Courtney. He'll be selling gold label award winning wines within the next few years, if it even takes that long. He's a brilliant entrepreneur and loves the challenge of making a business thrive. Driven is what he is, that's why he's never been married, or had time for a special lady in his life."

"I didn't know."

"It concerns me that he'll become a lonely old man if he doesn't slow down soon."

Jerry left the subject there, took his glass of red wine and got comfortable in the lounge room. Courtney cleaned up and pondered the insight she'd had into Kate Smythe.

Perhaps I can be more tolerant now. She didn't get the children she wanted and I didn't get the parents I needed. Sometimes life can be cruel.

There was a slip of paper under the back door; Millie had left another telephone message. It was usually Jacob Hoyle trying to contact her with the latest in the process of dealing with the banking issue. This one was a message from the Mt Barker Tourist Bureau. Courtney wondered what they wanted with her. She popped over to Millie's later in the afternoon.

"Hello, this is Courtney Lancaster. I received a message to call you back."

"Yes, Miss Lancaster, thank you. We're hoping you might consider taking in some guests from time to time when the other people are not occupying your guest room."

Courtney was caught off guard, but then remembered it was a small town. Everyone knew what was going on. She'd temporarily forgotten that bit of information. She responded, unsure about the suggestion.

"I'd have to give it some thought."

"Please do. There isn't enough suitable accommodation in town and your guest house would be ideal for people passing through the area. We'd appreciate the opportunity to send some visitors your way."

"I'll get back to you and let you know soon."

The conversation ended and Courtney was surprised to find herself considering the idea. It would be another source of income, especially once Keith's arrangement finished up in a few months time. She actually liked the concept, and she'd be hard pressed to find a guest more difficult than Kate to deal with.

"My guest house," she voiced aloud. Millie turned her head to look at her.

"What did you say?"

Courtney's face softened and she smiled.

"I have a guest house. That's what the Tourist Bureau called my place."

"Oh, I do like that. Courtney's Guest House, it has a nice ring to it."

"I prefer Lancaster House – in honour of Uncle Geoff."

"That's even better. So tell me more," Millie prodded.

They discussed the pros and cons and the outcome was that she needed to make her own space and the guest spaces separately lockable. She decided she would pursue the idea. Keith would be pleased, she was sure of it after her chat with Jerry. Now Todd would have to come and do a bit more work at her place. She made another phone call before she went back home to her 'guest house'.

"Brilliant idea," Keith enthused.

"I thought you'd like it."

"It will mean you can continue to work from home. If you can manage it, you could even squeeze in a part-time job."

Courtney screwed up her face.

"No, I don't want to do that. I love being here and there is plenty to do. Todd's going to work on some more renovations for me. I've managed to save enough to afford doing up the kitchen."

"If you need more money, just ask."

Keith was sincere, but he'd already done enough in Courtney's estimation. He didn't want any repayments for the original loan yet and encouraged her to develop this new opportunity.

She glanced across the table at him while he sat sipping his black coffee. He lifted his eyes and caught the look.

"What?"

"Nothing." She shrugged her shoulders.

"That's what my sister used to say. I never believed her and I don't believe you, either."

Courtney flushed with embarrassment.

"Well, I, it's just that ... I don't know how to say it."

"Just spit it out, however awful it might be."

"It's not awful. I was just wondering why you wouldn't want to have, you know, a lady friend."

"No time."

"Don't you think it might be a good idea to make the time?"

"No-one around to interest me, sorry. What about you, ever had anyone special in your life?"

She flushed again. Touché. She dropped the subject and talked about something else. The redirection of the conversation was not lost on Keith. It left him thinking about what might have transpired in this young woman's life that she hadn't shared with him, yet.

CHAPTER 11

The first day of spring arrived and with it came a fresh outlook for Courtney. The sun shone through the wispy clouds as she walked down the path to check the mail. A large beige envelope had been folded in half to fit into the letterbox; the return address was for Hoyle and Hoppman.

Courtney sat on the top step and took a deep breath of the crisp air. She appraised her front yard where the manicured green lawn and weeded garden beds were a stark contrast to the view she was greeted with on her arrival six months previous. A satisfied smile lit her face before she carefully opened the packet to reveal several legal documents.

A certified copy of her full birth certificate and driver's licence was attached to an affidavit from The Scarborough Hills Home for Children, Sydney advising of the error in their records of her incorrectly spelt surname as Lancashire. A shiver ran through her at seeing the name of the Home in print. Jacob Hoyle had forwarded proof of her identity to the Agricultural Bank in Perth and her bank account had been re-instated.

"Yes! Thank you, Mr Hoyle."

He'd done it, he'd fixed the problem. She relaxed. It felt good to be relieved of the monetary issue hovering in the background of her life. A sense of victory pervaded her thoughts, and a visit to the bank would be taken with relish.

She looked down the path at the roses which had begun to stretch dark red healthy shoots off their branches. It was an art lesson observing the pruning process by Maureen recently.

"You have to remove any dead wood, and all the weak ones," Millie's friend explained as she tugged away at the thorns caught on her leather gloves. "Then you prune these canes at least by half."

Courtney was amazed at how much Maureen cut the tall stems back.

"Sharp secateurs are essential, and they need to be kept clean." She shared how her father had been an avid gardener in his day and insisted on cleaning the equipment so it didn't spread disease from one plant to another. "Make the cut on a slight angle, not flat and not too sharp either. It has to be near an outward eye to encourage the new growth away from the centre of the plant."

"Why?" Courtney had no experience with roses, only weeding in the garden at the Home.

"To let plenty of light in there, it helps to keep black spot at bay."

"What's black spot?"

"It's a nasty fungal disease that makes black spots on the leaves and turns them yellow. Pick off any leaves affected by it, and those that have fallen on the ground, too. Mix some baking soda with warm water and a little bit of detergent to spray over the plant. Put some on the soil underneath, as well. That'll help to treat it and keep the plant healthy."

"How much baking soda should I use?"

"Just two teaspoons to about five litres of water should do it."

Maureen didn't have to think about measuring quantities, she'd been doing it for years.

"Make sure you water your roses in the morning so the leaves are nice and dry before nightfall. They like some fertiliser when they're flowering too."

"So many things to remember."

"Just check with Millie, she's good with roses. I think she wanted you to get to know people better. I'm sure that's why she asked me to come and help you." Maureen put more trimmings in the wheelbarrow. "Millie told me you're going to have other guests stay here."

"Yes, that's my plan. I'm going to call it Lancaster Guest House."

"Well done. Good on you. Did you know the first Inn[3] at Mt Barker was not far down the road? In Marmion Street, but it's just a ruin now."

"I might go and take a look sometime." Courtney smiled at the woman as she packed up her gardening tools and left by the front gate. *Older people are so interesting, always willing to share a gem or two of information.*

---

3 Old Bush Inn

Courtney approached the bank building with a bounce in her step; she looked forward to facing off with Gordon Prescott. The withdrawal slips were in their wooden slot at the bench, and she took one to fill out the details. Courtney stood tall in the queue waiting for her turn at the only teller booth open. The young man took her form and bankbook and completed the transaction without a hitch. She'd half expected a refusal but it didn't come.

"Can I see Mr Prescott, please?"

"Sorry Miss, he's not here."

"When will he be back?"

"Miss Lancaster, he won't be back. He's been transferred to the Perth branch in not too pleasant circumstances, if you get my meaning."

"Oh, well, can I see the new manager?" Courtney felt cheated of not getting her day of reckoning with Prescott, but there was a hint of triumph at the innuendo given by the teller.

"Yes, Miss, I'll let him know you'd like to see him. Just one moment, please."

A stately gentleman approached the counter; he put out his hand in welcome toward Courtney. She took it and offered a firm handshake.

"Come into my office, Miss Lancaster. Please, take a seat." Courtney sat on the seat he directed her toward.

"Thank you. My lawyer contacted me and explained that arrangements have been completed in regard to the issues I was having here."

"Yes, our bank offers an apology for the manner in which you have been treated. Mr Prescott has been reprimanded for his behaviour, and I can assure you there will be no problems from that perspective again. He is a desk clerk in the city branch where they can keep an eye on him."

After a short discussion she left the bank, pleased to be of acquaintance with the dignified Mr Alain Mitchell.

Keith turned up on Monday wearing work clothes, not his smart trousers and a button through shirt with a tie. Courtney wasn't surprised he'd come to visit but rather at his unusual attire. He explained he'd come to help Todd rip out the old kitchen cupboards and fit the new custom-made pine timber ones. They needed to get the job completed before Thursday when Kate and Jerry would be back. Keith didn't mind getting dirty and enjoyed the challenge of turning his hand to a new task.

The old chipped and worn cupboards had been dragged outside. They'd pulled up the linoleum that was to be replaced and discovered old newspapers from 1953 underneath. The three of them sat on the floor reading out the news of the day from the different editions of the West Australian.

"On May 29, Sir Edmund Hillary and Tenzing Norgay reached the summit of Mt Everest. They were only there for fifteen minutes before they had to start going back down again, otherwise they would've frozen to death."

"Mine says that oil was discovered in Exmouth in December."

"Where's Exmouth?" Courtney enquired.

"Up north," the men chimed in together.

"In Queensland?"

"What? No, north-west of Western Australia." Todd rolled his eyes.

"Well, I didn't know that or I wouldn't have asked." Courtney glared at him.

"And this one says Queen Elizabeth II had her Coronation in Westminster Abbey, on the second of June."

"Hey, the Perth drive-ins were showing Peter Pan, From Here to Eternity and Gentlemen Prefer Blondes with Marilyn Monroe. Do you think men really prefer blondes?"

"Ash blondes are the nicest ones," Todd threw a smile at Courtney.

"Ha ha."

"Here's a local paper, The Albany Advertiser." She flipped through the pages. "This advert says you can choose all your knitting accessories at Foys."

"Foys? Oh, that's in Albany, it was where David Jones is now, in York Street."

"Ah-ha." A mischievous grin spread across Courtney's face as she looked directly at Todd.

"Show me," Todd demanded.

She pulled the paper away and handed it to Keith. He glanced to where she pointed then looked at the younger man with a grin as well.

"What?" Todd was anxious to know what they were on about. Keith read out loud.

"Birth Notices:

York, Todd Aloysius

David and Helen welcome with love a son; born on 18th May at 4.30pm, 8lb 4oz.

It was very civil of you to arrive in the afternoon."

Todd groaned.

"1953 makes you sound very old. And Aloysius - nice middle name," Courtney laughed. As one could well imagine, Todd hated it. He pretended to be stern.

"Right, I think we've wasted enough time and we'd better get on with the job here."

"Keith, you'd better do what Todd Aloysius York says, he's the boss you know."

"Funny girl," Todd retorted.

Well, she thought she was funny.

The water had to be turned off to disconnect and remove the taps. Todd arranged for them all to go to Millie's place for lunch. By the end of the day they'd installed all the new cupboards with rich chocolate brown laminex bench tops that complimented the warm pine timber doors. It was a much better choice than the trendy orange or lime green colours.

A brand new stainless steel sink was connected with bright new taps that turned on and off easily. Courtney was thrilled but noticed that the old table and chairs looked very shabby by comparison; she could get a new dining room suite now that her money was available. Todd would take her into Albany to do her shopping on Wednesday providing he didn't hear his middle name again for at least a week.

It was late in the afternoon when they finished cleaning up the mess and they decided to order fish and chips. Keith had been going to leave until he heard this, and because it had been a long time since he'd had such a treat he chose to stay and join them. He didn't want to drive with the bright setting sun in his eyes anyway.

After a companionable meal together, they said their farewells and Keith headed back to Frankland River. The night sky was inky-black, dotted with bright stars and the ancient Milky Way galaxy a vast cloud band of light spiralling in the cosmos. Keith never failed to notice the austral array displayed in country skies.

He remembered his first encounter when he moved to the north of the state and discovered how majestic the stars appeared. They never looked like that in the city; there was far too much light for them to compete with and it washed out their beauty. He'd loved the cool inland evenings in winter spent sitting around a dying campfire and sleeping rough in his canvas swag. Memories of the clingy red dirt, stifling hot days and sweat trickling down his back in the height of summer were the things he didn't want to recall. His life could have been different if he'd chosen another path back then, but he had no regrets.

He'd enjoyed his time spent with the young people today. Maybe that's what it might've been like if he'd had adult children. They were bright, fun and hard-working. He would be proud of them if he was their father. Keith was pleased Courtney's bank issues were resolved and he was trying to think of a way to tell her not to worry about repaying the loan. He wanted to give the finance as a gift, but he knew that would upset her. She was fiercely independent and would insist on paying him back.

He'd have to think of something ... a shadowy movement caught his eye. He hit the brakes but it was too late to avoid a collision, the car smashed into a kangaroo and a loud bang reverberated in his ears. His head hit the steering wheel and he heard a snap of bones as the vehicle ground to a halt on the road. Pain flooded through him. Hot blood poured down his face and his heavy breathing hurt with each gasp. Keith was reluctant to get out of the car even though he could move his legs. He knew he was in shock; he felt cold and clammy but didn't pass out.

An overnight freight truck coming from the opposite direction witnessed the accident in his headlights. The driver pulled over and jumped out.

"Hello, can you hear me?" he called out as he opened the door.

"Yeah," was the mumbled response from Keith.

"Okay mate, just hang in there. Don't try to move, I'll radio for an ambulance and I'll be back in a tick." Fortunately, this was a regular run, and he knew approximately where they were located. He ran back to his truck, contacted someone to call 000, and grabbed a blanket from the cab.

"Here we go, are ya still with me?"

"Yeah, I'm cold ..."

"Let's put this around you, and keep talking to me. Where does it hurt?"

"Everywhere, but this is excruciating," he pointed to his right shoulder where the seat belt remained tightly strapped.

"Probably broke something. You hit a huge boomer."

"Did it survive?"

"Nah, it's well and truly dead. Thankfully, I'd hate to have to be the one to put it out of its misery. I'm going to put a couple of reflector signs out as a warning to other motorists, we don't want anyone else coming along and ploughing into both of us."

The truckie came back and used a clean rag to wipe some of the blood out of Keith's eyes and away from his mouth while they waited.

An hour felt like an eternity in the middle of the night. They heard the ambulance siren blaring before the flashing lights came into view. No-one else had come past in the time they'd been there. The paramedics checked Keith's pulse, blood pressure and asked several questions before they got him out of the damaged vehicle. It hurt but it was a relief to have someone who knew what to do. They gave him pain killers and oxygen and drove Keith to the hospital in Mt Barker.

CHAPTER 12

The clatter of a trolley in the corridor roused Keith from his drug-induced slumber. It took a few moments to remember where he was and what had happened. His tongue was dry and his lips were split and swollen. He wanted some water. He tried to lift his head off the pillow but a sharp pain shot through his ribs. He gave up and made sure he didn't move again. The aroma of food from breakfast trays being distributed to the other patients made him feel sick. A nurse noticed he was awake when she entered the room.

"Good morning. How are we today?"

Obviously, I'm not in the best of health.

"Water, please." The words rasped their way out of his throat.

She held the cup with a bent straw to his mouth and then wiped a wet cloth over his lips. It felt good. He sighed, then winced in pain.

"The doctor is doing his rounds. He'll come and speak to you soon." Keith nodded.

The nurse placed the buzzer beside his left hand and gave instructions for him to press the button if he needed anything. Keith's right arm was bound in a sling and he could see bruises on the back of his hand. The events of the previous evening swamped him, moisture gathered in his puffy eyes. *Like I need this right now,* he thought, but realised there could never be a right time. Fortunately, no-one else was in the accident. He remembered a truck driver helped him and wondered if he could be contacted.

A middle-aged man came in and chatted to the others in the ward. The stethoscope around his neck was the only indication he was the doctor. He approached Keith.

"Mr Crawford," he paused while he checked the chart at the end of his bed, "a nasty encounter with a kangaroo, I believe."

Keith nodded.

"Your blood pressure has stabilised, but your temperature is still slightly elevated. Can you tell me what level of pain you're feeling?"

"I'm aching all over. I can hardly move without this awful pain across my chest."

"Yes, the x-rays show a clavicle fracture and broken ribs. You may have whiplash, too. No other internal damage though. We can give you painkillers but there's not a lot else we can do other than keep up the cold packs and remind you to breathe as deeply as you can. It might hurt but we don't want you to end up with pneumonia."

Do all the staff here speak in the third person? He wondered about that but nodded in understanding.

"The sling will help prevent the collarbone from moving and that will cause less pain and help it heal more quickly."

"How long?" Keith managed to whisper. He was tiring.

"At least six weeks for the bones, possibly longer. How old are you?"

"Forty, this year."

"Mmm, and in good health, but that can be detrimental. We don't want to try to do too much too soon, or it will slow down the process. Do we get my meaning?"

"Yes."

"Do you have someone at home to help take care of you for the next few weeks?"

"No, I live alone."

"Okay, we will have to find a solution to that problem."

"I'll be able to manage."

The doctor raised an eyebrow.

"You'll need assistance to dress and undress and shower for a while, and you won't be able to drive for at least a month. There will be physiotherapy sessions to attend soon."

"Oh," another deep sigh, and that hurt too. *I guess I will need help, but who do I ask?*

"I'll send the social worker to speak to you. We'll keep you here overnight to keep an eye on you and we'll make arrangements for your release from hospital tomorrow. Try and eat something and keep your fluids up. We don't want you dehydrated."

The doctor took his leave.

There was a loud banging on the back door with Millie's strained voice calling out.

"Courtney, Courtney."

"What is it? Are you all right?"

"Yes, no! It's Keith. I just got a call from a friend who said Keith's in hospital."

Courtney paled.

"Why? How come? What happened?" All these questions tumbled out.

"He's been in a car accident. Last night, but apparently he's okay, just badly bruised and a few broken bones."

"It must have happened on his way home after he left here. Was anyone else hurt?"

"No. He'd hit a kangaroo and then a truckie helped him out."

Courtney stood wringing her hands together.

"What should I do?"

She was completely at a loss to know but trusted Millie's judgement.

"Get yourself cleaned up and I'll take you to the hospital to see him. It should be all right to go now, it's already after ten. That's when visiting hours start."

"Okay."

The young woman was shaken. *It could have been much worse. What if he'd died? Thank you God that he hasn't been seriously injured.* Courtney exhaled a deep sigh of relief.

An orderly assisted Keith to sit up and slide his legs over the edge of the bed.

"That's good. Just sit there for a minute and rest," a nursing aide instructed him. "Now try and stand. Take it easy, we're here to help. Are you sure you won't use the urinal bottle?"

There was no way Keith was using one of those things, or a bedpan either. He didn't care how much it hurt; he was going to the toilet. The orderly gave him his arm to hold onto while he shuffled like an old man across the corridor to the men's bathroom. When he went to wash his one free hand Keith was shocked at his reflection. Swollen black eyes looked back at him through the narrow slits; a wound above his right eye had seven stitches in it and his face was covered in bruises. He held onto the bench to steady himself.

"Are you ready to attempt going back?" The orderly had been waiting for him. Keith nodded and they took their time to return to his lowered bed. He was thoroughly exhausted by the time they had lifted his legs and tucked him back in again.

Millie went to the enquiries desk and found out which ward and bed Keith was in. At first the antiseptic smell hit their senses, and then the sound of beeping machines and soft-soled shoes squeaking on the shiny linoleum floors echoed in the passageways. The ward nurse smiled at them when they arrived. Millie let her know they had the room number they needed. It was dimly lit and the six-bed ward had four curtains pulled back, but Keith's was partially closed. He was asleep. Courtney gasped. A single tear ran from the corner of her eye and slid down her cheek. She didn't know what to expect but her reaction took her by surprise.

"It's mostly superficial, love."

Millie took Courtney's hand in her own and squeezed it.

"Poor fellow, that's a deep gash on his forehead. Here, you sit on that chair and I'll go get another one. Be right back."

All business-like the older woman took charge. It wasn't pleasant going to the hospital and visiting the sick but she'd done it many times over the years.

They sat for a while in silence, and Courtney suspected Millie was praying. Keith's eyes flickered and opened.

"He's awake, Millie."

At the sound of her quiet voice Keith turned his head in her direction. He attempted to smile but was unsuccessful. He moved his hand to reach out and Courtney took it. Her lips wobbled as she spoke a shaky hello and fresh tears escaped while she dabbed at them with a tissue. He cleared his throat to speak.

"I'm okay, just very sore."

"And we can thank God for that," Millie piped up with cheerful banter.

Keith nodded his head in agreement. A nurse came to take his observations and record them on the chart. She offered him a warm cup of tea with a straw.

"I'd love a coffee, black with some cold water."

"Coming right up, sir." She left to get it for him.

"Sir ..." he re-iterated and did the thumbs up sign.

"Well, you haven't lost your sense of humour," Millie chuckled, "that's still intact."

They helped him sit up a bit more, wincing along with him at every movement. He took the drink and relaxed a bit. *It's so good to have such caring friends,* he thought. They were here before he'd even had a chance to let them know.

Todd came flying down the passage and into the ward, his hair swaying in his eyes.

"Oh, thank goodness. I thought you were on your death bed, but here you are drinking coffee with company." He grinned, but genuine relief could be heard in his comments. "So tell us what happened."

Keith managed a brief version of the accident and asked them if there was some way they could find out who the truck driver was. Todd said he'd ask around.

A tray with a bowl of clear soup and a square of jelly with custard sat on the table in front of Keith. He didn't think it looked very appetising but he was feeling hungry. Just reaching for the spoon was an effort but he was determined to manage until he spilled it down his front. Courtney took pity on him and offered to feed him. He was embarrassed but accepted her help. His face hurt with each mouthful and he was glad he didn't have to chew it. Swallowing was difficult enough.

After he'd eaten some lunch they went off and left him to sleep with a promise to return later. Millie said she'd dig out some pyjamas that had been Harold's once. They'd wash up well, and Keith could use them instead of the hospital gown he was wearing. The three friends left to have lunch themselves and discuss what course of action would be needed in the short term for Keith's convalescence.

CHAPTER 13

Grey-faced, Keith walked out of the hospital foyer after his ride in a wheelchair to the front door. The seat in the red utility was pushed back as far as it would go. Keith could get into it much easier, and with a lot less pain, than trying to fit into Millie's little Datsun 120Y. Arrangements had been put in place for the injured patient to stay at Courtney's with help from a Silver Chain nurse to sponge bath and change him for the next four days. After that, Todd would help with the ablutions around his work commitments.

The drive from the hospital to Lancaster Road was far enough for Keith. He felt quite ill even in that short distance. *Here I was thinking I'd be able to look after myself.* He objected when they led him into the main bedroom.

"But I can't stay here, this is Courtney's room."

"I need to be able to hear if you need help, and I can't do that if you're in the guest room. Todd got a new mattress for the single bed in the other room and I'll be comfortable enough. You'll need the extra space in here for when the nurse comes."

Courtney was firm in her manner.

"Besides Jerry and Kate will be here tomorrow, unless you want to cancel them coming this week."

"Yes, I mean no. Oh, I don't know."

He hated being confused.

"Have a rest and I'll make some lunch in about an hour. We can talk about it then."

She walked out and let Todd help him take off the dressing gown Millie had also given him. Keith sat on the side of the bed. Todd looked at the strong man stricken with incapacity, and realised it was a humbling experience for him.

"You'll be okay, Keith, just one day at a time at the moment. Won't be long and you'll be back to your old self again."

"Yeah, thanks." Tears welled in his eyes. "Sorry, I just feel so useless."

"That's because you are ..." and Todd laughed.

It made Keith want to laugh too but he grabbed his rib cage, screwed up his face and pushed out a puff of air.

"Don't make me laugh, it hurts."

Todd helped him lie down propped up on several pillows.

A decision to ask Jerry and Kate not to come for two weeks was made by mutual agreement between the foursome. Millie took the phone number and the responsibility of explaining the situation to them. It was too soon for Keith to think about work and Courtney needed to focus on taking the best care of him.

The vineyard was in the early stages of bud break and providing there was no frost they'd be fine. A couple of weeks could be spared before the quick growth would require vine training to develop the correct canopy for fruiting.

"Your car has been taken to the panel beaters. The assessor will decide if it's worth fixing or just write it off. Oh, and I found out who the truck driver was." Todd directed his conversation to Keith.

"He's a fellow from Mayne Nickless, Tom somebody-or-other. The truck depot owner knows of him. Nobody is sure of his surname but we've left your message for him to contact you."

"I'd rather thank him personally, if I can. I should have come in the one-tonner on Monday; at least that's got a roo bar. Maybe things wouldn't have turned out like this."

Keith took his medication and went back to bed. It had been 36 hours since the accident and he was sore and bone tired.

The nurse was with the patient, so Courtney took the opportunity to take a hot coffee onto the front verandah and have some time for herself. The last few days had been taxing. Keeping cold packs, soft foods and medication up to the patient had taken most of her time. There was a marked improvement today though.

Keith had come out early at breakfast time and sat at the kitchen table, the old one because no furniture shopping had transpired since the accident. His face was a mosaic of yellow and green with a few smudges of purple. His swollen eyes had returned to normal and the wound on his forehead was healing well. He could manage doing a few things himself, using his left hand, after a bit of practice.

Millie went off to church and Todd was going to call in later. A refreshed Keith came out with the nurse and they waved goodbye. A look at her cup indicated his desire for a drink.

"Coffee?"

"Yes, please. I want to sit here too, it's nice to be outdoors."

They chatted about a few things and worked out what they would do the following week. A gentle walk up the road each day would help the healing process and get Keith out of the house. Courtney insisted that she should go with him the first time to be sure he would be all right on his own.

Todd volunteered to go out to the property at Frankland River and get some clothes and paperwork Keith needed. He'd accepted that he would have to stay in town for a while. He had an appointment at the doctor's surgery for the stitches to be taken out on Tuesday, and a physio consultation on Friday.

"Tom, there's a message for you," the office girl pointed to the pin-up board in the corner where several bits of paper had been skewered with a push pin. He found the right one and read it.

"So, have you been moonlighting, Tom?"

His boss peered at him through squinted eyes.

"No. Why do you ask that?"

"Well, that message looks like you're about to be paid off with some big bucks. Who's gonna do that, hey? You been using my runs to take your own freight around the state?"

"Absolutely not, this is about that fellow I helped on the road last week. The one that hit a roo down south, remember."

"Oh, yeah. Okay."

Tom didn't take kindly to the insinuation that he would do the wrong thing. That wasn't like him at all. He might have the appearance of a rough truckie with his long greying hair, bearded face and tattooed arm but he was as honest as the day was long.

He'd try to work the job so he could visit the address at a reasonable hour next week when he was on that run. Probably on the return trip would be best. He went home and told his wife about it. There was a phone number to ring the next door neighbour, and she suggested he call the day before to let them know he was coming. Annie was usually right about these things. Tom thought he'd better do it.

The table was covered in paperwork. Courtney couldn't understand how Keith knew what was where, but he seemed to.

"No not that one, the one over there."

She passed the document to him. He read it.

"Okay, so write this for me."

Courtney took the dictation on scrap paper and then wrote it out on the letterhead for Crawford Estate Winery. She didn't have a typewriter and didn't know how to use one very well. Keith said a handwritten letter would be fine, and he'd commented that she had lovely writing. It was something she'd always been proud of, and he couldn't write left-handed so the task fell to her.

They worked all morning at his business and after lunch Todd helped Keith shower and shave. He was spent after the physical and mental exertion and went to lie down leaving the young people to themselves.

"I saw this dining room table and chairs in the paper for sale at Lockes in Albany," Courtney showed Todd the picture. "I like it, and it's in my price range."

She looked at him with an angelic smile. He got her drift.

"So, you'd like me to go get it for you?"

"Oh, would you? That would be very nice of you to do that for me." She laughed.

Todd was going to take Keith to the doctor in the morning and said he'd go to town afterwards. He left re-assuring her the furniture would fit on the back of the ute and he wouldn't need to take the trailer.

Courtney was excited at the prospect of getting her new dining suite. She'd stacked the crockery and kitchen utensils onto the melamine shelves in her new cupboards. Todd was going to make some open shelving on either side of the chimney over the stove, a place to put her recipe books. It had become a favourite pastime, reading them and trying new ideas. Some of the experiments weren't so good but mostly they turned out just like the pictures in the books.

A sleepy-eyed Keith came out about three o'clock in the afternoon.

"Wow, I really bombed out, didn't I?"

"You must have needed it."

Courtney held the gate open for Keith and he stepped down to the footpath. He took a deep breath, felt the distinctive twinge but a sense of freedom enveloped him. This was a good thing to do. They talked while they walked to the post box on the corner.

Keith shared some of his background, about growing up with Jerry and how they were the best of friends even though they were from different social classes. Jerry's family were in the wealthy part of Subiaco and Keith lived in the state housing flats. They had attended the same schools and studied at the University of Western Australia. Jerry did a double major in Science and Agriculture and Keith took on Engineering under a well-earned scholarship. The young men enjoyed many escapades together and travelled around the state picking fruit or any job they could find in their uni breaks. They knew each other inside out and were still good mates even with the difficult situation of Kate in their relationship.

"I never knew what it was like to have close friends," Courtney lamented, "until I came here."

"But you must've had kids around you all the time at the Home."

"Yes, but that was different. Most of them came and went, some were fostered out to families and the little ones were often adopted. I was always the eldest and usually ended up looking after them. There were older boys, though, not so many people wanted boys."

"You've had it tough, Courtney."

"Yeah, but look what I've gained. It was worth the wait."

She continued to tell him in more detail about Uncle Geoff's gifts in the wardrobe; about the contents of the trunk and how she was able to remember a bit about her parents now. Keith shook his head.

"Well, I never would've believed it. That's incredible. I'm happy for you."

They'd arrived back at the house and walked up the path to the front door. Courtney felt a delicious warmth encircle her heart. She couldn't believe it either, at times, but it was all true.

CHAPTER 14

Tom drove straight to the post office and entered the push door of the public telephone booth. He dialled home.

"Annie, you're not gonna believe this." He related the conversation he'd had with Keith Crawford just minutes before.

He rang the bell on the front door of number 16 in Lancaster Street. Tom felt nervous but wanted to make sure the man in the accident was getting better. He waited. A young woman answered the door which he didn't expect. He thought it would be a middle-aged lady.

"Tom? Come in," she invited him in at his nod and stepped inside. They went down the passage to the kitchen. He was glad he'd rung to let them know when he was coming.

"Keith, this is Tom — your rescuer."

"Don't get up on my account." But it was too late, Keith already stood with a beaming smile across his face.

"Thank you, thank you so much for all you did for me last week. I can't tell you how grateful I am."

He shook Tom's hand, as strange as it was, with his left hand.

"You're welcome, mate. Only did what any decent person would do."

"But not everyone is decent, someone else may have just driven on by."

"A Good Samaritan ..." added Courtney. They'd had a discussion about that in the Ladies Bible Study group. They both looked at her, and nodded in unison. "Can I offer you a cup of tea or coffee. I have lemon barley cordial in the fridge if you'd prefer a cold drink."

"I'll go the cordial, thanks." Tom pulled out a chair with a dark blue and pink floral cushion and sat at the new pine table.

"So how did you go? You still look a bit battered."

Tom assessed the fading bruises and the arm in a sling. Keith enlightened the interested visitor about his injuries and his healing progress.

"I start physio this week and once I've got the ability to raise this arm a little, I'll be right to head home the week after."

"Where's home? I thought you lived here." Courtney and Keith exchanged an uncertain glance.

"I live in Frankland, that's where I was heading when the kangaroo jumped out in front of me. So, tell me a bit about yourself. How long have you been driving trucks?"

"Pretty much since I got a licence. My old man was a truckie and I guess I just followed in his footsteps. It's an okay job but it's not the best for family life. You know, being away a lot and getting up early and home late but Annie, that's my wife, she's a gem. She just soldiers on and manages most of the family by herself."

"How many children do you have?"

"We got three young kids, two boys and a girl of our own, and there's my older step-daughter who doesn't live at home anymore. She's Annie's girl."

"I guess life could get easier if you had a different job."

"Yeah, but drivin' is all I know."

"What would you say to considering the idea of a new job opportunity?"

"Meaning?" Tom frowned.

"Maybe you might be interested in coming to work for me at the vineyard in Frankland River. It'd be a better life for your family. The job would come with a four-bedroom house, no water, power, rent or rates bills. There's a primary school in town and the bus goes straight past the property."

"I don't know nuthin' about growin' grapes."

"But you know machinery, engines and such, I'm sure. You'd be able to drive anything and mow grass, pull wire fences and look after the property." Keith persisted.

"Always service me own truck, love fiddling with greasy bits and pieces. My Annie, she knows grapes, she grew up in Margaret River. Spent years pruning and picking."

"Well, there you go. What do you say? Would you think about it? It would be $15,000 in wages per year with extra money for Annie if she wants to work in the vineyard, and that would only be if she wants to do it."

"You're kidding me! That's $5,000 a year more than what I earn now. You're sayin' that all those other things go over and above like?"

"Yes, that's what I'm saying."

Keith was enjoying this.

"Well, I'll be danged."

The man sat there silent for a time.

"Why would you do this? I mean, you don't even know me. All I did was help you when you was in need. I really don't get it." He shook his head.

"I know you are respectful and have sound ethics, Tom. I need a caretaker at my property but I need someone in a hurry. Would two weeks be too soon? Would Annie agree to it?"

"Bloody oath. She'll be happy to get out of that city and live in the country. My boys would love it, too."

They all smiled at that comment.

"I'll tell you what, Tom, go talk to your wife and give me a ring in two or three days and let me know what you think. Ring that same number you contacted us on before. Millie will pass on a message."

"Okay, and I reckon it'll be a done deal." They shook hands again and said farewell.

Tom left the place with a weight lifted off his shoulders. They'd been struggling lately and he wasn't happy in his job at Maynes'. But so soon? Annie might not want to pull up digs and move that quickly.

It was silent on the other end of the phone. Tom got worried, his Annie was never short of a word and here she was speechless. A cough escaped through the lump lodged in her throat.

"Annie, are you all right?"

"Yes," she whispered, "I can't believe it, Tom. It's just what we need, I told you God would provide."

"You did at that, my love."

"When can we move?"

"I take it that's a yes. Do you want time to think on it? Maybe, pray about it too?"

"I've been doing that already, Tom. It's the answer I've been waiting for. You agree, don't you?"

"Yes, yes I do. Will the kids be okay about it?"

"I don't see why not, they'll make new friends. Better ones, I suspect. And Freya will just have to accept our decision, not that it will make much difference to her anyway. She's determined to do her own thing at the moment."

"I'll let you sleep on it. I'll be home tomorrow and we can talk about it then."

"I'll start packing," Annie said and hung up.

CHAPTER 15

Courtney looked at Todd, her eyes intense and head tilted to one side. "How come you don't go to church?"

"I do, every week." Todd responded calmly.

"I haven't seen you there."

"No, that's because I go into Albany."

"Why? Wouldn't your parents like you to go to church with them?"

Courtney had met Helen and David York the first time she went to All Saints. Millie had introduced her to them.

"Yes, I'm sure they would but I like going to the other one. It feels like my spiritual home."

"What does that mean?"

"Well, it's where I feel God wants me to be for several reasons. I think it's important for me to be in a place where I have my own identity; where I can learn about my walk with the Lord with the guidance they have to offer me; I like the different style of presentation, and I get to go for a surf after church."

"Aha, there's the rub."

"No, not really, it's just an added bonus. Sometimes I get invited for Sunday lunch by different families or couples. I enjoy that, getting to know them better. I know everyone here and I grew up with the same customs. Not that there is anything wrong with the formality, it just doesn't suit me as well. Do you know what I mean?"

"I think so." Courtney considered Todd's opinion.

"You'd better go see if Keith's ready for you to dry him off."

Tom, Annie, James, Jonathan and Bronte O'Reilly drove up the long driveway of the vineyard and parked near the front door of the large brick and tile house. The truck was loaded with their furniture, personal belongings and many pot plants. Annie was a bit of a green thumb and enjoyed gardening. They had always rented, so she kept special plants in pots to take with her when they moved house.

Keith heard the truck and saw a station wagon pull up. He went to greet his new employee and meet Tom's family. He was surprised to learn that Jimmy and Jon were energetic eight-year-old twins. Their golden haloes of hair and blue eyes favoured their mother's colouring and it was difficult to tell them apart. One had a smattering of freckles across his nose which was the only obvious difference. Little Bronte was four, and cute as a button with a head of curly red hair and dark green eyes. Annie was a lovely, wholesome woman in about her mid-thirties. Tom was older. Keith thought he was much closer in age to himself.

They received a warm welcome and went into the tiled entry that led to an open-plan kitchen, dining and family room. A carpeted, separate lounge room and big bedrooms with a huge bathroom left Tom and Annie gaping in wonder. They'd never lived in a house like this before. It was spotlessly clean and ready for them to move in.

"The house is only five years old. It was built by the previous owners, they planned to build a cellar door but didn't get that far before they had to sell up. Their baby had a serious medical condition and they needed to be close to Princess Margaret Hospital in Perth. I bought it about a year ago." Keith continued, "I had my young friends, Todd and Courtney, come out to clean the place yesterday. It wasn't too bad, but I needed to shift into the cottage over the way and with this arm I couldn't do it by myself."

"You moved out for us?" Annie was shocked and upset. She went to protest, but Keith cut her off.

"This is far too big for me," Keith explained after noticing the look on her face.

"I wanted to go into the cottage anyway, it's much more comfortable for one person. You have no idea how much of a relief it is to have you all here."

The children had begun to thaw out and explore the rooms while the adults talked. It made Keith happy to hear their excited voices. The boys were on school holidays and this was a new adventure for them.

"After you've unloaded the furniture and sorted yourselves out a bit, we'll go to Mt Barker to stay the night. We've set up a couple of extra folding beds in the guest room at Courtney's for your family and I'll use the other spare room. We have a feast ready to celebrate your arrival. Well, Courtney and Millie have been cooking for days. There's enough food to bring out here to use while you unpack. Tomorrow we can come back and you can get yourselves settled into your own place. I hope that's all right."

"All right? Man, we feel spoilt rotten."

Tom went to shake hands vigorously but remembered in time about Keith's injured arm.

"How's it going now?"

"Much better, just need to be a bit cautious. Thanks."

Dinner at Courtney's was lively. The children loved their gifts from Millie, she'd given the boys a dinky car each and a Little Golden Book to Bronte. There was a great deal of banter and discussion about teaching the children to beware of snakes in the coming summer, of going to catch yabbies at the dam and riding bicycles around the property.

One of the first jobs Keith wanted Tom to do was to build a lean-to down at the gate where the boys could leave their bikes for when they caught the school bus. The other mums in the district only drove the kids down to meet the bus when it was raining. Jimmy and Jon looked forward to it, in Perth they were only allowed to ride their bikes in the park when Annie was with them. Now they could ride everywhere. They were rapt.

Bronte sat on her mother's knee for most of the night, a little shy of the new people around her. Courtney tried to talk to her but she turned her face into her mother's shoulder.

"Sorry," Annie was a bit embarrassed, "she's not particularly social, not at all like her brothers."

"Well, that's not surprising, is it love? She's lucky if she can get a word in," Tom added with a chuckle.

He was glowing, Annie had never seen him like it. What a blessing this was, a new job, a new home and new friends. She praised God in her heart all the way to the property the next day.

There was a knock at the front door, it was nearly 9.00pm. Courtney debated whether to respond or ignore it. Jerry and Kate were out in the back room, so she decided to see who was there. A tall man with a fawn-coloured Akubra stood in the circle of porch light nervously turning the broad brim round and round in his hands.

"Sorry to disturb you Miss, especially at this late hour, but the fellow down at the pub said I might be able to get a bed here for the night. They're full up with Main Roads fellows for the week. My truck broke down, and it won't be ready until tomorrow afternoon. I need somewhere to have a quick shower and sleep."

Courtney took a long moment to consider his request.

"I do have guests already, and that room isn't available but I have a small single room you could use for one night. Okay, come on in. I'm Courtney."

She smiled at the man. His calmness and deep voice gave her a sense of certainty that he could be trusted.

"Thanks, thanks so much. What a relief, I thought I might end up on a park bench. I would've slept in the truck, but its up on the hoist and I can't reach the cab door. My friends call me 'Jarvo', and I promise I'll be out of your hair in no time tomorrow morning."

She showed him to the room, it was small but clean, and she'd changed the sheets after Keith had left the other day. Jarvo used the bathroom and went straight to bed. The following morning Courtney noticed his door was open, the bed made and money left on the little table. He was gone, without even having breakfast.

CHAPTER 16

Telecom insisted that she wait for the new push-button phones to be delivered before they would connect her to the system. In the meantime, Courtney had to continue being reliant on Millie for messages and making calls. It wasn't the inconvenience or the privacy that upset her, it was the fact that the company was being stubborn about the issue. It didn't matter what sort of phone she had, she just wanted one.

Millie's message to ring Jacob Hoyle at a different number sat on the table, he asked her to ring at 11 o'clock this morning. She took the note and went over early to visit her neighbour before it was time to make the call.

"Hello Mr Hoyle, I received your message. I hope to be able to give you my own phone number soon. I'm waiting on Telecom for my connection."

"That will be wonderful, Courtney. I'm in Perth for a conference and I'd like to make the trip south to visit you. Would that be all right? I'd need to stay for a night, and I'm hoping Friday will be suitable."

Courtney considered using the room that Jarvo had stayed in but felt it wasn't adequate for the solicitor. She decided to put him up in her own room instead.

"Certainly, Mr Hoyle, I will look forward to seeing you. I have other guests staying but that won't be a problem. How are you getting to Mt Barker?"

"I'm hiring a car and will leave after lunch on Friday."

"Great, I'll expect you for dinner then."

They said their goodbyes.

Millie looked at Courtney for details.

"He's coming to stay on Friday. I wonder why? Do you think there's a reason behind it?"

"I guess you'll have to wait and see. Could be, but it might be to make sure you're managing okay. Remember, he has had an interest in your life since you were a child."

"True, I hadn't thought about it like that." She remembered something else. "Did I tell you a man came to stay last week? He called in late and wanted a bed for the night. I put him in the single room."

"Was that wise?" Millie looked concerned.

"I was a bit reluctant at first, but Jerry and Kate were there. And, I sent up one of those quick prayers you told me about. I felt sure it was safe. He was a pleasant fellow but he left early. He said his name was Jarvo. Quite mysterious really."

"My goodness, you are becoming an astute business woman."

"I'm loving it, thanks to you and all your help."

"That's what friends are for."

Kate was out in the field taking photos of the vines where fresh new growth burst out and twisted along the bare wires. Curling tendrils reached for something to grasp and the light green rows of grapevines stretched across the landscape contrasting to the loamy soil beneath. Close-ups and panoramic views filled her roll of 24-shot film. She wanted to document the progress from bare branch dormancy to fruiting with plump bunches of grapes hanging beneath green sawtooth leaves.

It would be useful for the brochure to promote Crawford Estate Winery from Frankland River within Australia and overseas. Kate had read an information pamphlet earlier to get an idea of what the district offered.[4] An excellent winery was just what the area needed to attract more people. Crawford Estate could provide that and she was going to make sure everyone knew about it in the future.

They'd met the O'Reilly family when she and Jerry arrived this morning. Peeved that they were a permanent fixture at the property, she decided to escape in the vines with her camera. Kate could hear children's voices. She looked up to see the boys riding their bikes and little Bronte sharing Jon's seat hanging onto the crossbar for dear life. It looked a bit precarious to Kate. Jimmy helped her off when they reached the perimeter of the dam. They had nets to catch yabbies.

Neither of the boys were watching their little sister, so intent on putting the bait in the nets they didn't see her wander down to the

---

4 Frankland River

water's edge. The clay on the steep bank was slimy and Bronte lost her balance and slid in. The water was freezing cold and took her breath away. She couldn't even scream for help.

Kate was witness to this and the boys were oblivious. She pulled off her shoes and jacket, dropped her camera on them and ran flat out to rescue Bronte. James and Jonathan were surprised to see the lady running toward them. When they realised what had happened Jimmy started yelling.

"Swim, Bronte, swim."

But all she could do was splash around and gasp for air before she went underwater again. Jon began to cry.

Kate jumped in and pulled the little girl out, tipped her over and tapped her back to make her cough up the water she'd swallowed. She vomited and looked at Kate, terrified from her experience.

"It's all right, pet," Kate crooned, pushing her wet red curls away from her face and caressing her little body with light strokes to calm her down. Bronte allowed her to hold her close.

"Boys, one of you go and get my jacket from over there and one of you ride back to get help. NOW!"

Both boys jumped to and did as they had been commanded. Jimmy rode his bike faster than Jon, so he told his brother to get the jacket. Kate wrapped Bronte in it and began to stride out for the house. It was more than a kilometre away. Jon ran alongside, sobbing all the way.

Annie drove in the direction that Jimmy pointed out until she saw Kate and her daughter.

"Mummy ..." Bronte whispered between hiccups. She took her little girl and Kate drove them back to the house.

"What the hell do you think you were doing?" Tom raged at his sons. "You didn't ask if you could go, and to take Bronte ... well, I can't believe you'd do something so stupid." The twins stood with their heads down, their bodies shaking with fear.

"Tom," Annie interrupted quietly, "I think they've learned their lesson."

"I want to belt them within an inch of their lives, their sister could have drowned."

"They know that, Tom. Look at them, they're just little boys being children. They didn't intend for Bronte to get hurt, and I'm sure they're sorry. Boys?"

"Yes, Mum. We just wanted to show her the yabbies. We didn't see her go away from us." Jimmy explained.

"I'm sorry, Mum and Dad," Jonathan was on the verge of tears again. "I couldn't bear it if she drowned and it was our fault. I'll never do anything like that again, I promise."

Tom's heart melted, they were adventurous spirits but young and vulnerable. He put his arms out to them and they fell into their father's embrace. The family stood together and gave thanks to God for his protection, and for Kate being there to help, and the chance to learn from what had happened.

Kate watched the drama unfold and marvelled at the parents' wisdom in dealing with the situation. She was drawn into understanding the O'Reilly couple from a new perspective.

Annie gave Bronte a warm bath and Kate had a hot shower. Annie offered her a Target brand tracksuit to wear. Kate didn't mind because it was warm and dry. Her clothes were saturated. Annie handed Bronte, wrapped up in a big towel, to Kate and gave her a hairbrush. Bronte had said it was okay for Kate to do her hair.

After gently untangling the mass of curls, Kate dressed the little girl in her favourite pink butterfly pyjamas while her mum cooked some soup for lunch. Bronte was tucked into a blanket on the couch. Kate read several stories until her little eyelids drooped and she fell asleep. Auntie Kate - her new name, was thrilled with being involved and thanked Annie profusely for allowing her the privilege.

It was the topic of discussion at the dinner table that evening with Kate, Jerry and Jacob sharing the wholesome meal Courtney had prepared. Courtney was impressed to see Kate glowing with a happiness she'd not seen before and with a completely different attitude. The conversation diverted to many subjects and it was long after the meal that they were still sitting in the kitchen.

"Courtney, I'm pleased you've done so well with Geoffrey's legacy. You should be very proud of yourself."

Mr Hoyle was generous with his comments and Courtney took the compliment to heart.

"Was there something in particular that you've come all this way for?" She had to ask.

He paused and passed a glance at the other guests. They took the hint and excused themselves.

"There was something I wanted to tell you in person. I discovered how Gordon Prescott knew about your identity issue." Courtney directed her full attention to what he had to say.

"My partner, you know, the Hoppman of Hoyle and Hoppman, had inadvertently told his wife about your situation. We realise it was a breach of confidentiality but Alistair thought it harmless enough at the time. However, he was unaware that his wife's childhood pen pal is Gordon Prescott's sister. She wrote in one of her letters that she knew you were living in the same town where Gordon lived and described how wonderful it was that you had a positive turn-around of events in your life. She also mentioned about the name discrepancy at the Home and how things could have been quite different if you'd been found sooner. Her friend passed the information on."

Courtney took in the statement. Jacob waited for her to respond, somewhat fearful of the repercussions to the blunder made by Alistair Hoppman.

"What are the odds of that happening? All I can say is 'it was meant to be.' If that hadn't happened, I wouldn't have met Keith and the Guest House wouldn't have evolved and I've realised that God has plans for me in spite of how they emerge. It was frustrating at the time, but I see how it has worked out for the best in the end."

"Do you want to pursue the company's breach? You have a legal right to do that."

He felt obliged to let her know.

"No, of course not. You were unaware of the situation, it wasn't your fault and you've been a great help through all of this. I have no intention of making an issue out of it. I've had enough of those lately. I'd say it appears to have been an innocent remark that Prescott used to his own advantage. Not that it did him any good."

She shared the demise of the former bank manager with Jacob.

"I did come here to be sure you are well and settled. I see you are, that and more. I think I'll take myself off to bed now and I'll see you in the morning."

"Good night, Mr Hoyle."

"Jacob, please. Call me Jacob."

CHAPTER 17

A slip of paper under the door read - MBTBx1MxW@4?Mxx Millie's notes had become quite the algebraic phrases. The poor thing, it must be so annoying to be interrupted with all these calls. *Next week, Millie, the phone will be here.*

Interpreted: Mt Barker Tourist Bureau, one man on Wednesday at about 4pm, Millie xx

Courtney would be ready to receive the visitor. It would be busy on Thursday now with changing sheets and cleaning for Jerry and Kate to come later that day. She would have to make sure she did as much cooking as possible on Wednesday morning. Courtney sat down to plan meals and write a shopping list.

There was the knock on the door, not the ring of the doorbell. Courtney hung the damp tea-towel over the warm stove rail and went to answer it. She was pleased everything on her list was ticked off.

She stood there, door open, stiff and unresponsive.

"Liam ..." the whispered name slipped from her lips.

"Hello, Courtney."

The handsome young man wasn't surprised at the reaction. He knew she would be shocked to find him on her doorstep. The tell-tale habit of running his hand through his wavy hair when he was nervous didn't go unnoticed by Courtney.

"I'm your guest for tonight."

"Oh," she saw he had a bulging overnight bag. "You'd better come in then."

Her confidence flew out the window, this is not what she expected the afternoon to bring. Dare she ask what he was doing here? In her heart she already knew the answer but didn't want to face the truth. She showed him to the guest room.

"I think I deserve an explanation. Don't you?"

His open face wasn't condemning but concern and confusion lingered there.

"Yes, you do but I'm not sure I can give it to you."

She walked out. *Breathe, just breathe.* Courtney let out a huge breath. She attempted to avert a panic attack but was shaking and a sheen of sweat droplets gathered on her arms.

"Oh, God, what am I going to do?"

Be honest, a still small voice came to her mind. She hadn't experienced that before, but knew it was a response to her prayer. *I can't … it's too hard.*

Yes, you can, I am with you wherever you go. You are not alone. God was with her, she felt His presence and knew from the scriptures that she could do all things through Christ Jesus who would give her strength. She decided to pray in her room with the door closed.

Dinner was ready and Liam sat at the table opposite Courtney. He asked if he could give thanks for the food, and she nodded in agreement.

"Heavenly Father, we thank you for the food you have provided and the opportunity to be together today. In Jesus name, Amen."

He deliberately kept it simple. He didn't want to frighten her with the diatribe in his head and heart. They began to eat in silence.

"How did you know where to find me, or are you here for some other reason?"

Courtney had been wondering about this since Liam arrived and curiosity provoked the conversation.

"I'm here for you, this is not a coincidence. I made a missing persons report with the police after you disappeared. I checked all the hospitals in Sydney first in case you'd been hurt and couldn't contact me. I was worried sick but waited until you should have returned to work and when you didn't turn up, I went straight to the police. I imagined all sorts of horrible things, thought you'd been traumatised by some evil intent or murdered."

"I'm sorry, Liam. I panicked and ran, it never occurred to me how you would feel. My own struggle didn't allow me to think beyond myself. I wanted to write to you, but every time I tried nothing made any sense. So I didn't do it."

The young man held his tongue, he couldn't understand her behaviour; his emotions were raw and just below the surface of control.

"It took some time to trace you, and by the time I'd found an address you'd gone again. I never imagined you would go interstate."

Courtney explained how her windfall had transpired and about the life she had built here. A gentle light shone in her face, one he'd never noticed in the short time he had known her. While it hurt that he'd been left out of the equation, he was glad to see her unreserved happiness. They did the dishes together and Courtney bid Liam goodnight.

She went to her room and battled with the emotions his presence had stirred up. It was a restless night, crying and praying and confusion rivalled each other for a place in her thoughts. She woke after a few hours sleep but felt tired and emotionally drained. *Breakfast, go and face it,* she pushed herself to get to the kitchen. Liam was already up, and sat at the table with his Bible open, reading in Psalm 119. He looked up.

"Good morning."

His benign greeting fell on deaf ears.

"What would you like for breakfast?"

"Just some toast, thanks."

"I have fruit bread, white or wholemeal. What would you prefer?"

"The fruit bread sounds good."

Courtney's hospitality mode kicked in and she bustled about getting food ready.

Liam asked if he could read aloud. Courtney felt obliged to agree. He began from verse 142, and continued to the end of the chapter.

"Your righteousness is everlasting and your law is true.

Trouble and distress have come upon me, but your commands are my delight.

Your statutes are forever right; give me understanding that I may live.

I call with all my heart; answer me, O Lord, and I will obey your decrees.

I call out to you; save me and I will keep your statutes.

I rise before dawn and cry for help; I have put my hope in your word.

My eyes stay open through the watches of the night, that I may meditate on your promises.

Hear my voice in accordance with your love; preserve my life, O Lord, according to your laws."

Some of the verses caught her attention. Maybe he'd had a bad night as well, and Liam intended for her to hear these words. She knew it would be his tactful way of saying something without actually voicing what was on his mind.

Fearful of broaching the real topic of discussion that was needed, their conversation danced around the edges of it until the time Liam was due to leave at 10 o'clock.

"I'm not ready to go yet, Courtney."

She knew why, and he was right.

"I have guests coming this afternoon."

"Do you have another room?"

"Yes, the small bedroom is available but the bathroom is shared."

"That's fine by me, I want to stay."

"Okay, but I'll be busy all day."

"Whatever is needed, and however long it takes ..."

Liam looked at her, their eyes locked and she melted. She'd deliberately avoided those beautiful brown eyes for hours.

Kate and Jerry arrived early. Fortunately, she'd remade the bed and cleaned the bathroom in time. Kate came into the kitchen loaded with parcels, rolls of bright wrapping paper, scissors and sticky tape and dropped it all on the table.

"I'm so excited. Courtney, come and see what we've got for the boys."

She stopped and looked at the younger woman.

"You did get invited, didn't you?"

"To the twins 9th birthday party? Yes, Kate, I think Annie invited us all to the barbeque after school tomorrow."

"Oh, thank goodness, I thought for a minute I'd made a big faux pas. Are you okay?"

It was not like Kate to be bouncy or thoughtful of other people's feelings. It came as a surprise to Courtney, she nodded that she was all right, even though she was on shaky ground.

"I didn't want to wrap these up before I showed you what we bought."

Jerry came in, rolled his eyes and shrugged his shoulders behind his wife's back.

"She's got a new focus, Courtney, these kids have stolen her heart. I just hope I get to keep a corner of it for myself."

Kate nudged him with her elbow, and gave him a quick hug. They were looking at the Lego train sets when Liam walked in.

"Kate and Jerry, this is Liam. He's staying here too."

"Nice to meet you," Jerry smiled at him. "I had a train set when I was a kid, it wasn't Lego though. Keith and I spent hours playing with it. We used to make our own little houses and shops for a town, and we had farms with toy animals in matchstick fenced paddocks. Brings back great memories."

The men picked up the boxes, one was an Inter-City Passenger Train set and the other was an Electric Goods Train set; they discussed the challenges of building with Lego bricks.

"I thought they could be combined if Jimmy and Jon want to make one big set, it's up to them. And look what I got for Bronte … I know it's not her birthday, but I can't give the boys something and not have anything for her."

She pulled a Cabbage Patch Doll out of another bag.

"Which means you'll have to do the same for the boys when it's Bronte's birthday," Jerry commented.

"Yes, I know. It's so much fun. I love it." Kate beamed.

The gifts were wrapped and cards attached. They cleared the table for dinner and shared a meal before retiring to the lounge room for a chat before bed. It was all very cordial and a relief to avoid facing a one-on-one deep discussion with Liam.

The breakfast dishes were done, floor swept and the washing was in the machine. Courtney had just sat down for a coffee with Liam when Millie came over to bring a message from Annie. She'd sent word to invite the guest along this afternoon. Courtney was disappointed by the offer. *I thought I'd be able to escape to the party early and now Liam will probably come too.*

Millie stayed and Liam was quizzed about where he was from and what he did. Millie learned he'd grown up in Sydney and was a high school teacher at a co-educational school. The washing machine finished its cycle, Courtney excused herself and left them chatting. She did have concerns that Millie might probe too far, hence the washing was hung on the line very quickly.

The conversation ended as she came back into the house. They were smiling and saying farewell until later in the day. Liam had accepted the invitation to join them, and arranged to take Courtney with him in the hire car.

On the drive to the vineyard, Courtney explained who Keith was and when they'd met. She told him about the accident and how Tom, Annie and the children came to live and work at Crawford Estate Winery recently. It slipped out about Kate and Jerry and the relationship they had with Keith before she realised she probably shouldn't have said anything. It was easy talking with Liam, and she'd missed that.

Courtney gave him directions as they drove through the Frankland River township towards the property. Liam offered the 'don't blink or you'll miss it' joke about the size of the town, being city kids they marvelled at the number of small isolated towns in Western Australia. Everyone else had already arrived, not that they were late because Liam was a stickler for being on time.

The front door was adorned with a blaze of bright coloured potted petunia. Annie welcomed them into her home, it was no longer a shell of a house. She had made it into a homely haven. They walked through to the family room where clouds of balloons floated upon twisted blue and white streamers.

There were hugs from the boys when Courtney gave them their gifts. Bronte stayed sitting on her Auntie Kate's knee. Everyone looked toward the couple, and Courtney introduced her companion.

"This is Liam Wilson, my husband."

The silence was fractured by soft gasps. Odd expressions passed over the faces of the adults. Todd quietly voiced what everyone else thought.

"You never said you were married."

"No, I didn't."

Liam's heart did a back-flip, he wasn't expecting her to be brutally honest. It was a good step in the right direction.

Annie took control of the awkward situation.

"Right, boys, do you want to play pass-the-parcel or musical chairs first?"

"Pass-the-parcel," they echoed in unison.

The tension broke and the children became the focus of the evening.

CHAPTER 18

The yellow beam from the headlights illuminated the long gravel driveway. Liam concentrated on avoiding potholes, and rabbits that darted across their way. His passenger was slumped down in the bucket seat beside him. Courtney wanted to leave early from the twins' birthday party. It had been a taxing time for her after the abrupt announcement she'd made. At the intersection to the main road, Liam paused and let the car idle.

"That was brave of you. I didn't anticipate you'd say anything."

"Well, it's true."

"Yes, it is."

Silence.

"Are you okay?"

A shadowy shake of her head was all he could see. He reached over and took her hand, and that was her undoing. A deep sob escaped from her lips.

"Oh, Courtney, it's all right."

"No, it's not ..." she mumbled, emotion tying her vocal chords in knots.

"Let's get you home."

A nod this time.

"Be careful," Courtney whispered, "this is the road Keith had his accident on. Watch out for kangaroos."

Liam hadn't done much country driving and kept his speed below the limit in case he needed to brake in a hurry. They drove on, quiet with their own thoughts until she relaxed.

"You've made some great friends, Courtney."

"They are, and I can't believe the difference in Kate."

"She barely took any notice of Keith. After what you'd told me, I thought there might be some uncomfortable moments."

"There were."

"Uncomfortable moments?"

"Yes, but that was because of me, not Kate. Sorry to embarrass you."

"I wasn't embarrassed, but I don't think your friends knew how they should react. Did anyone say anything to you?"

"Millie and Todd did," she paused. "They both said I could have told them."

"Why didn't you?"

"I was too ashamed about the way I'd treated you. It had been hard work to push it all aside in my mind where I don't deal with feelings. And in the last six months I've had to face things I didn't even know were there. Now I'll have to do it again."

It went quiet, and Liam was unsure of whether he should broach the issue they needed to discuss. The rubber tyres rang their rhythm of revolution against the bitumen road bringing them closer to the township of Mt Barker. The confined space in the small vehicle felt safe, like a capsule cushioning them in absolute privacy and isolated from other intrusions. Perhaps it was the right time and place to begin the conversation they had to have.

"Why did you leave?"

Liam braced himself for what might come.

"Because I'm not good enough for you."

His head jerked left.

"By whose estimation do you base that on?"

"My own."

"Did I do or say something that made you think like that? If I did, I'm sorry because it's not true."

"It wasn't you, it's me."

"Why? I want to understand but you're going to have to explain it to me."

He held the urgency of his plea in check struggling to maintain an even tone of voice.

"Please?"

"I don't know if I can."

Her voice was soft and strained.

"But there is a reason?"

"More than one."

She was silent for a time. Courtney wanted to talk it out, but how could she? It would expose her in a light she'd attempted to avoid thinking about since she was fourteen. Old recriminations surfaced, memories and images flooded her mind. She shuddered.

She couldn't speak, turmoil raged within, she wanted to tell him but it just wouldn't be verbalised. Tears filled her eyes, anguish left her rattled. Liam sensed her conflict. Many minutes passed, Courtney took a deep breath, the knife-edge of nerves in her voice sharpened as she began to talk.

"In 1974 the Home allowed some volunteer helpers to throw a New Year's Eve party for us. Families were invited to come and the room was crowded with a lot of people we didn't know. Davey was one of the older boys at the Home. He was really good-looking, you know, the black hair, dark blue eyes, chiselled cheekbones and chin. I think he had a Celtic heritage. He was watching me, and I got the same tingling sensations I'd felt a few times before when he was close by. I knew he liked me, well, I thought he did. His eyes always followed me around the room and he'd push in to stand behind me in the queue at the cafeteria. I'd feel his warm breath on my neck, and his skin would touch mine when he reached across to get a plate. It sent shivers through me. We rarely spoke to each other but there was a magnetic attraction I didn't understand."

Courtney stepped back in time in her mind's eye. Liam prayed for her. *Lord, I don't know where this is heading but it doesn't sound good. Please give Courtney the courage to keep talking and give me the wisdom I need to know how to respond.*

"Davey asked me to dance. He was excited. We moved to the beat of the music, laughing and having fun. I felt free from the boredom and routine of our regimented life. The record player belted out Blue Suede's song Hooked on a Feeling. We sang the words ... *'I'm high on believin' that you're in love with me.'* I thought this must be what love feels like; my heart was bursting with pleasure. The countdown to midnight began and on yelling out 'Happy New Year' Davey kissed me. It was a sweet kiss, then he held my hand and we ran out the back door into the cool night." There was no going back now, Courtney spilled out her story. Liam listened.

"I felt happy until he pushed me against the rough brick wall at the back of the toilet block. Davey held my head, his fingers twisted through my hair, pulling at it while he pressed hard kisses against my lips. I was frightened. Everything was spoiled. I could hardly breathe with his face crushing mine. He was hot and sweaty. He put his hands under my shirt and unclipped my bra, his kisses went down my neck and he held my breasts. I said to stop but he wouldn't listen. I was crying but Davey didn't care."

"Then he unbuckled the belt in his jeans, I was so scared I tried to scream but he put his hand over my mouth. A dull light flashed around the corner, and Davey took off. The security guard was doing his rounds. I stood there by myself with my arms folded across my chest, shaking and breathing fast."

"Did the guard have any idea what was going on?"

"No, his torch flashed toward me, and he said I should know we weren't allowed to smoke and told me to go inside. He probably thought I was scared at being caught out, but I was relieved he'd interrupted what was happening. I couldn't go back into the building, though."

"What did you do?"

"People were beginning to leave. The party was over, so I ran to my dorm."

Liam exhaled the deep breath he didn't realise he'd been holding. They drove into the driveway at home and parked the car but neither of them were in a hurry to get out. They sat in the dark and continued to talk.

"I felt sick and dirty. I wanted a shower but I knew Matron wouldn't have let me, and I didn't want to explain anything to her. I ran hot water into the basin, soaped up a flannel and washed the saliva and sweat off my face and neck. I still felt him on my skin, so I used more hot water and soap and scrubbed harder. I did the same with my arms and breasts. My face was red raw. My tears stung on my cheeks."

Courtney swallowed to moisten her throat.

"It was my own fault, I should never have gone outside with him."

Liam was furious.

"That boy took advantage of your innocence. And, you asked him to stop! It wasn't your fault, and you didn't know what he intended to do."

"But I was too weak to even fight him off."

"Of course not, you were in shock, and the creep had you pinned to the wall."

The bright lights of Jerry's Mercedes revealed hazy silhouettes of the couple in the hire car. A tiny rivulet of gathered moisture from the condensation on the rear window trickled down. The interruption caused an awkward moment and Courtney stopped talking.

"Looks like they're making-out," Jerry chuckled.

"More like making-up," Kate corrected. "And don't go banging on the car or tapping on the window either. Leave them alone."

They walked past arm-in-arm to their room at the back of the house. Courtney's teeth began to chatter, her folded arms didn't help alleviate the chill she felt.

"Shall we go in?"

"What if they're in the house? I don't want to see them."

"I can go and check," Liam offered.

"No, please don't leave me by myself. We can go in the front door. I have a key."

Her hands shook as she tried to open her handbag. Liam wrapped his coat around Courtney's shoulders as they approached the house. It was quiet inside. He led her into the lounge room, sat her down on the sofa and put a rug over her knees. She was motionless, eyes glazed over, tear stains on her cheek. Liam lit the fire and went to the kitchen to put the kettle on. He slipped into praying again.

Lord, I can't believe what she's been through. She's lost both of her parents; had to grow up in an institution with no family or friends, and now I find out she's been abused as well. How can I help her? I love her even more for being open about the things she's hidden away for so long.

It explained some of her reactions that he hadn't given much thought to before. He understood why she'd flinch when he put his hand on her back when she couldn't see he was going to touch her. And why there were times she had deliberately distanced herself from him.

The fire crackled in the grate, flames licked the soot-covered alcove. Warmth began to fill the cosy room, and Courtney rested in the comfort of it. The dark thoughts she'd carried for years felt less burdensome. Liam returned and handed her a mug, she wrapped both hands around it, and sipped the hot liquid. He sat on the floor with his own cup and looked across at her. She smiled at him weakly.

"Is there more to tell, or have you had enough for now?"

"I need to keep going, I don't want to hold this in anymore."

Liam added more wood to the fire and stirred the embers.

"I didn't sleep much that night, the whole thing kept going round and round in my head. The next morning Matron called me into her office. I was scared she'd heard something about the night before. She looked up from her paperwork, saw my face and asked why I was so red. I told her I got sunburn the day before and she accepted that as the reason. Matron wanted me to take the toddlers out to the sandpit while she interviewed some parents who were going to adopt a baby."

Courtney put the empty mug on the table and rubbed her hand over her face.

"It took a week for my skin to return to normal. I hated myself, and every time I looked in the mirror I shuddered. Davey turned 16 in February and the rule was that we had to leave the Home on our sixteenth birthday. He had gone, and the continual reminder of what happened on that night went with him. I decided to bury the shame and hurt deep inside of me. I didn't want to ever think about it again."

"But you did on the night we were married? Did you plan to run when you went down to the car to get your bag?"

Liam needed to know.

"No, not until I went outside in the dark and cold. I noticed the red brick walls of the building, and it took me right back there. I got frightened and felt dirty again. I didn't want you to touch me. I'm so sorry."

The rug slipped onto the floor, and Liam stood to pick it up. Their eyes met and they held each other's gaze. Courtney recognised the compassionate understanding Liam had for her.

She saw the handsome groom at the altar waiting for her. His father walked her down the aisle to meet him. The veil over her face couldn't hide the smile she wore. They exchanged their vows and rings, and she was happy when people threw confetti over them outside the church. The reception was wonderful and she'd been welcomed into Liam's family with open arms. It had been after midnight when they left for their hotel room in the city. They'd filled out the breakfast menu and hung it on the outside of their door. Her forgotten overnight bag was in the back seat of the car, and Liam offered to get it but she wanted to do it herself because there was a gift in it for him she didn't want him to see. Then it all went horribly wrong.

Liam had put the television on and sunk onto the couch while he waited for Courtney to come back. She seemed to take a long time; relaxed in his contentedness, he fell asleep.

She'd panicked; hot, dizzy and short of breath Courtney had leaned against the door of the car. Memories flashed through her mind, she was tainted and Liam deserved better. She unlocked the car, grabbed her bag and in an instant decided she had to leave. But where? This was Sydney after midnight, and she had no-where to go. The 24-hour reception desk light flashed, and she had cash in her bag. Pretending to be calm she went to the office and booked herself into a room a level up from the one Liam was in. She paced the floor until dawn.

When Liam woke suddenly, he realised where he was and was annoyed with himself. This was his wedding night. What was he doing sleeping on the couch? Courtney wasn't in the bed, or in the bathroom. Where was she? He began to think something must have happened and ran down the stairs to look for her. The car keys were on the seat. It was a miracle it hadn't been stolen. Her bag was gone.

He felt sick, and looked between the parked cars for her. He searched in the alleyways and back streets. She was nowhere to be found. Perhaps she'd been hurt and someone had called an ambulance. Liam was shattered. He jumped in the car and went to every Accident and Emergency Department of all the nearby hospitals but no-one answering Courtney's description had been treated during the night. He was beside himself and rang his Dad. He needed the older man's wisdom and a shoulder to cry on.

Early morning sun shone through the orange net curtains in Courtney's hotel room. She stood at the window and watched the car park below. Liam had returned and collected his things from their room. She didn't know where he'd been but noticed his distressed behaviour from her perch above. Guilt brushed her conscience, but she couldn't do anything about it, she had to escape. There was a bus stop across the road, and she would go wherever it would take her.

"You said there was more than one reason ..." Liam sat beside her but kept a safe space between them.

"I realised after I left you that I wasn't good enough for God or you. I thought I could be like you and your family but I only had a surface understanding of God. I didn't trust anyone; in my mind God took my parents, didn't protect me from Davey, and you were too good for me and deserved someone better. I'm not sure my faith is what it should be, you're so confident in what you believe. I think I'm searching for a true belief in God, that's what Millie says I'm doing."

The fire had burned down and a pale light appeared in the window. They'd been up all night. Liam wanted to pursue the subject she'd just raised but he thought better of it.

"And that's what God hopes for us, that we will look for Him. Just so you know, none of us, including me, is good enough for God but we'll talk about that tomorrow."

"Oh, that's right, it's already tomorrow."

She smiled at his attempted humour, and agreed it could wait. Liam said goodnight, and they went to their own rooms.

CHAPTER 19

Reverend RJ Webber's study felt safe. The young couple were seated in comfortable chairs at the massive English oak desk. A light green IBM electric golf ball typewriter sat to one side with an inserted sheet of foolscap paper. Probably Sunday's sermon notes. Bob's room was lined from floor to ceiling with shelves bulging with all manner of books. A large family photograph took pride of place on the wall surrounded by small framed drawings of local native orchids.

He was a kind man with a wealth of experience in his chosen vocation. Reverend Bob noticed Courtney fidgeting with her handkerchief, and Liam's stiff countenance. He suggested they pray before beginning their 'journey of discovery', as he called their time together. Reverend Bob was going to set aside two hours every Wednesday for the next three weeks to spend with them. He'd already explained he expected them to be completely honest, listen to his recommendations and to carry out the after-session tasks he would set. They'd agreed.

"Heavenly Father, we come before you in sincerity and truth. We seek your counsel as we search for your will in these young lives. Lord, you already know their story and you have a plan for them to be reconciled in every way. Teach us, we pray, to be open to your guidance today. In Jesus name, Amen."

Discussion about their family backgrounds and up-bringing revealed much to Bob. Courtney's was quite a unique situation. Liam's solid Christian family life was healthy and happy. They did not go into depth about Courtney's experience with Davey. It was mentioned, but Bob felt it would be better to spend time dealing with it specifically at the next session.

The task for the week was to write a list of what was good about their childhood before they became teenagers; what they felt should have been different, and how they thought children should be raised in today's society. They were commissioned to go to a playground with a slide, swing and sandpit and to play together for at least fifteen minutes.

It didn't take long to talk about Liam's list, there were only a few minor negatives he'd felt while he was growing up. His belief in God didn't allow him much popularity when he was at a public school, but he was never bullied. He knew he was different and that wasn't always easy as a child. He had good memories of family holidays and a great relationship with his parents.

Courtney and Liam spent hours working through the shocking loss of her parents. All she could remember was being told they'd died in an accident and was sent to a family for a little while before going to the Home. Most of her memories were of being raised as a ward-of-the-state, but then she had the cherished revelations since being in Mt Barker. They recognised how an institutionalised upbringing didn't allow her to develop an understanding of who she was in her own right. They laughed about some things, cried about others and debated how they'd like to raise children themselves – one day.

The playground was free on Tuesday, they'd kept an eye out for a child free opportunity. It seemed a bit silly for adults to be there without children but they had a promise to keep.

"Higher, push harder," Liam called out.

Courtney gave him an almighty shove.

"That's better."

She hopped on the swing beside him, at least she'd had plenty of turns on the swings at the Home. It was one of the best activities they'd enjoyed, and when she was older there was often a child on her knee.

"I'm free," she called out as they sailed past each other.

Laughing felt good. Liam jumped off and left the swing gliding through the air, empty. He scaled the ladder and slid down the steep slide. Courtney joined him and they took turns up and down the slippery slope. The mid-afternoon sun caught golden highlights in her tangled hair.

"We should go to the sandpit now." Courtney instructed, sounding like the senior girl caretaker giving orders. "Let's go."

A built-in excavator caused some role-play fun.

"It's my turn now," Liam demanded.

"You have to ask nicely."

"But you've been on there for ages," Liam pouted.

"Can I please have a turn?" he whined.

"In a minute, I have to finish digging this hole."

"You're not fair." He sat down and folded his arms.

Courtney laughed out loud.

"You know, I never got to do that at the Home. We had to take turns without any nonsense or we got sent to our dorm and missed out altogether. That's a good thing I should put on my list, I didn't think about it before. Sharing and respect for each other was high on the agenda of good behaviour."

A sand castle towered in the centre of the sandpit. It had rocks for windows, sticks for flags and leaves for trees. Courtney and Liam looked at their masterpiece, very proud of it, and happy they'd found an old tin to bring water from the tap to moisten the white sand. Gritty hands, a touch of sunburn and a dose of good old-fashioned play had lightened their afternoon. Kids were coming on bikes to the playground; and since they'd been there for over an hour, they slipped off hoping no-one noticed them.

Bob sat at his beloved desk, it had belonged to his father before him who had inherited it from his grandfather. Generations of Webber men had scribed messages for the saints, read the scriptures and folded hands in prayer over the desk's timber grain.

He was a large man, with greying hair and deep furrows on his wide brow. Honest blue eyes shone below bristled grey eyebrows.

He'd spent the past week studying God's Word in relation to grace, forgiveness and healing. Bob had pored over the stack of books beside his bed on grief counselling and abuse every night before he'd turned his lamp off. There had been many occasions when he'd helped others in dire situations, but he felt a heavy burden for Courtney with her long-held suppressed memories.

"Are you ready for tomorrow, dear?" Beryl asked while she readied for bed.

She'd noticed her husband's withdrawn silence this week and was concerned for him.

"Yes, I think so. It's never easy talking to people about deep emotional issues, but I trust God for direction in our conversation. I just don't want to say the wrong thing."

He had confidence in his Lord, although there were times he felt quite inadequate. The mature couple spent time in prayer together, and fell into peaceful slumber.

Wednesday rolled around again. Bob welcomed the young people and they shared the insights discovered through the discussions about their childhood years. They'd had fun in the park and felt a bond grow in the carefree playtime.

The Reverend was pleased, and they were ready to forge into the difficult realm of the effects of abuse. Two hours later Courtney was aware that she was blame-free and had nothing to be ashamed of; her reactions were normal in the situation, and realised it takes time to build trust in people. She recognised Liam was a safe haven for her and not a threat, if she was struggling with her feelings and reactions it was important to say so.

Liam was encouraged to listen and watch for any triggers she might experience. They could work through it together, she was not alone and had his support in every way. A romantic date and measured physical contact were the essential steps to take in the week to come. Bob felt content that they were ready to embrace the slow processes needed to develop a healthy physical relationship.

Liam had booked a table at the Penny Post Restaurant in Albany. They were going on a date, a candlelit dinner with an à la carte menu. He'd bought flowers and decided to get chocolates as well. Courtney had changed three times before deciding that her Sunday best would have to do. She'd put her hair up and applied some make-up.

Nervous anticipation made her feel a bit giddy, but she looked forward to it. Liam's enthusiasm had been a delight to watch as he planned the occasion. He really was very sweet and she knew he loved her without question. *I hope I don't disappoint him again, I just want this to be a good night for both of us.*

Chivalry was not dead. Liam opened the car door and the door into the restaurant for Courtney, and pulled out the chair at the table for her. She kept laughing at him because it was not something men did anymore. Although Jerry did it for Kate all the time, but it seemed right for them. Perhaps it was their social status that made it appropriate. Liam had arranged for Jerry and Kate to have dinner at the winery so Courtney was free on Saturday night.

They'd chosen their dishes from the menu after the drinks arrived. A waiter with a white folded cloth over his arm came with a notepad in hand.

"What would Madam like to order?" the waiter asked looking at Liam.

"She'll have the Steak Diane and I'll have the Lobster Mornay, thanks." Liam responded for them both. They had a bit of a giggle after he walked away.

"Madam? Really? I've never been called that before."

"It's very posh for a country town."

Liam had dined with family and friends in Sydney restaurants where correct dining protocols were expected by the high class customers. Their food was delicious and dessert menus were offered. They declined, and Liam paid the bill. They wandered down Stirling Terrace to the car, holding hands.

"Let's go park somewhere and attack those chocolates," Courtney suggested.

"I didn't think you wanted dessert." He said as they got in the vehicle.

"I didn't. I wanted to share these with you in private."

He couldn't see it in the dark but knew there was a cheeky glint in her eyes. It's what they used to do when they'd started dating. He would pick her up from a late shift at work and drive to Mrs Macquarie's Point. It was a magical view of Sydney with the harbour reflecting red, white and yellow lights in its still or ruffled water. The illuminated bridge was a majestic sight framing the white sails of the Opera House from their vantage point. Courtney loved the tray of

Roses chocolates Liam would spoil her with, but it was always on the condition she shared them with him.

They parked at the Albany fishing jetty car park.

"You go first, Liam."

"No, that would be breaking tradition. It's your turn, I got first pick the last time we did this."

"You remember whose turn it was?"

"Like it was yesterday."

Courtney had been chatty, but she went quiet at his comment.

"Do you think we rushed things a bit?" she whispered.

"Probably for you, now in hindsight, I can see that. I was ready then and I guess I thought we'd spend the rest of our lives getting to know each other better. We've certainly learned more in the last few days than we knew a year ago."

Courtney selected a chocolate and passed the box to Liam. He picked one and they sat in silence eating the milky sweetness.

"I knew I wanted to meet you when I saw you from the checkout the first time I came into the store where you were working." Liam's sheepish grin surprised her.

"Is that why you came into the shop just before closing so often?"

"Yes."

"And you needed something from the shelf I was restocking?"

"Yep."

"How much stuff did you buy that you didn't need?

"Quite a bit, actually." He paused and smiled at her reaction. "I knew you were the girl for me."

"How could you know that?"

"It was deep in my spirit. I'd prayed for the right life partner for years, and no-one else came close. I would have dashed off with you straight away."

"On a white horse?"

She smiled and gave a short chuckle.

"Yep, if I'd had one. Maybe I should have done something about that then. It might have saved us a whole heap of grief."

"Sorry ..."

"You know, Courtney, nothing happens without there being a purpose in it. Whatever it is that we learn from this journey will make a difference, not just for us, but maybe someone else in the future."

"Liam, you're always so positive about everything. I love that about you, and I appreciate it in a new light now."

"What else do you love about me?"

His question was voiced so softly Courtney scarcely heard it.

"A lot of things ..."

A week later Bob was thrilled with the outcome of the couple's date. They spent time in prayer and shared scriptures to show Courtney how to grow her faith in God. Bob explained how necessary it was to extend grace to forgive those who had wronged her. It was a difficult step to take when no remorse was shown by the offender. Resentment had to be released for peace of mind, a peace that passes understanding that can only come from God.

Romans 8 struck a chord with her, she had been set free through Jesus' gift of his life, his death and resurrection. She had reassurance of hope for the future and accepted God's unconditional love and learned that nothing could ever take it away from her.

CHAPTER 20

The spring sunshine warmed Jerry's back while he bent over to take the final soil sample for the day. Kambarang was his favourite season, the days were becoming longer and there was less rain. He'd adopted the Noongar seasonal calendar for wineries in the South West some time ago. It was truer to the climate with its six seasons instead of the conventional four.

Sealed bags of the rich gravelly loam with identification markers for where he'd extracted the cores of soil were lined up on the back of the ute. In his mind he determined which tests to request, of course he'd need the soil pH value, potassium, nitrogen and maybe he should include magnesium as well. He had data records kept by the previous owner but wanted to be sure he had accurate and current information. Jerry loved the scientific aspect of his work.

He stretched and checked the time. Noon, excellent, he would join the others back at the house. Keith came out of the cottage when Jerry parked the ute. They wandered over to the house together discussing the previous year's vintage.

Annie usually prepared lunch for them all and they enjoyed sharing stories from their different experiences in life. The two men walked around the back to the patio door and noticed Annie and Kate sitting at the dining room table. The women were deep in prayer, heads bowed, oblivious to the time.

"What are they doing?" Keith didn't want to interrupt.

"They have a bible study together on Friday mornings."

"On my time?"

Keith had an annoyed edge to his voice.

"No, Keith, we're on an hourly rate remember. We only charge for the hours we work. Kate doesn't include the time she spends with Annie."

"I didn't mean to sound like that," he stiffened. "I'm surprised Kate's interested in what the Bible says."

"She's learned a lot here, and it's made a big change in her life."

"I did notice she was different."

Tom joined them.

"Why are you guys hanging around out here?"

Jerry pointed out the problem.

"Oh, let's go in through the laundry door and I'll see if it's okay to interrupt them."

They cleaned up at the trough and Tom came back and waved them into the house.

Bronte sat on the floor between Annie and Kate playing with her Cabbage Patch doll. Kate's eyes were red from crying. She approached Keith after having a quiet word with Jerry.

"Can we have a quick chat?" A nervous inflection sounded in her voice.

"Sure," Keith glanced at Jerry and received a nod from his friend.

"Outside, if you don't mind."

They went through the patio doors and stood in the courtyard still visible to the others but where they couldn't be heard.

"Keith, I'm sorry for my bad behaviour in the past. I'm embarrassed at the way I've treated you and I wasn't aware of how much it damaged your friendship with Jerry. Can you forgive me?"

Kate got the words out, she had to deal with this and it couldn't wait any longer.

"Of course, I can. I have to say you've changed, Kate."

"For the better, I hope."

"Absolutely, and I look forward to having the friendship we should've had a long time ago."

"Thanks, Keith." Kate smiled, relieved at dealing with her guilt, and they went in for lunch.

The pumpkin soup was served, fresh homemade bread was sliced and put on the table.

"Liam's going back to Sydney on the weekend," Jerry commented. "He's been off work on leave-without-pay for the last month."

"What's going to happen? Is Courtney okay?" Annie wanted to know if their young friend would need support in the days to come.

"I believe he's going to complete the term at his school in Sydney but will resign and return to WA before Christmas. That's barely six weeks away. Courtney and Liam have been counselled by Reverend Bob. I've got no idea of the details but I think she's in a much better place about everything that's happened between them now," Kate added.

"It's all a bit of a mystery, but it's their business and we don't need to know any more than what they're willing to share," Annie added.

Keith asked Tom to pass the butter and they exchanged a quizzical glance. Far be it for them to understand what was going on!

"Liam said it was a miracle he ended up with the same private investigator Jacob Hoyle used to find Courtney. He'd prayed about it and just chose a name out of the yellow pages in the telephone book." Jerry shook his head. "Apparently the lawyer felt compassion for Liam when he told him his story and Jacob gave her address to him. Not necessarily ethical but morally he couldn't deny him the chance to restore their relationship. Liam didn't want her to know he was coming."

Bronte interrupted the conversation when she knocked over her cup and spilled water all over the table.

"Sorry, Mummy."

"It's okay sweetheart, it was an accident."

Annie got a cloth to mop it up and the discussion turned to other subjects about work at the vineyard.

Liam had repacked his bag but was leaving a few things behind. He wouldn't need his jacket and jumpers in Sydney in November so there was no need to take them. The last few weeks had changed his life, again. At least he was comfortable with the outcome and was pleased he'd taken the plunge and come west. Liam was certain of God's direction in his life, and to move states would be a wrench from his family but the right move for Courtney. He'd find a new job next year.

His plane ticket needed to be collected from the travel agency in Albany. They'd planned a final outing before he left for Perth in the morning. A visit to The Gap in the Torndirrup National Park followed by a picnic at Lawley Park, then a climb up the steps to the Desert Mounted Corps Memorial on Mt Clarence.

The view across King George Sound was majestic. The couple stood hand-in-hand absorbing the beauty. Eclipse and Breaksea Islands were steep granite rock protrusions surrounded by dark blue water where manned lighthouses had stood in the past. Stunning Middleton Beach stretched out as a wide crescent of white sand that could be seen from their perch on the hill.

Liam and Courtney walked along a track to Padre White's lookout which took in the view of the town of Albany nestled in the valley below. The south-west was to become their home and the joint decision to begin a new journey together filled them with a sense of peace.

The loose gravel of the track on the way back down caused Courtney to slip. Liam caught her just before she fell and he held her in his arms. She relaxed and looked deep into his eyes. Love flowed from him, and she responded to his gentle touch as he ran a finger down her cheek. There was no rejection from her.

"Can I kiss you?" his voice husky and undemanding. Courtney nodded. It was a parting gift and a reminder for them both that they had a future to explore in every way. The tender kiss and realisation that they would be separated for a while left them both emotional. Descending the long staircase from Mt Clarence was made in a comfortable silence. They were looking forward and not back at past experiences. The difficult days would be worked through with God's help.

"They say absence makes the heart grow fonder," Liam quoted the next morning as he hugged his wife before getting into the hire car to return to the capital city. "I've stored up these last few days in my memory to see me through until I get back. I'll ring you after I arrive home, I'm glad the phone's in and we can talk whenever we want. 'Bye Courtney."

"Bye, I love you."

Liam melted at her words, smiled and sang *'To God be the glory'* all the way to Perth.

CHAPTER 21

atteries, don't forget the batteries. Todd kept reminding himself because he'd already forgotten to get them twice before. He arrived at the Co-op and saw Annie come out of the automatic sliding doors pushing a trolley full of shopping.

"Hi, Annie and Miss Bronte."

Bronte smiled at him shyly. Todd deliberately felt all of his pockets, and with a teasing look at her, revealed a packet of lifesavers. Bronte's face lit up, she was expecting a sweet treat from him. He always had one for her.

"There you go, little lady."

"You spoil her, Todd."

"Yeah, I suppose I do."

A loud voice called out.

"Mum ..."

Annie turned to respond to the girl who appeared behind her.

"Freya, this is Todd, a friend of ours," Annie introduced her daughter.

The blood from Todd's face drained and he went chalk white. A very pregnant Freya stood before him.

"We've met before, Mum." Freya smiled at him.

Struck speechless, Todd swallowed.

"Oh, where was that?" A surprised Annie asked.

"In Margaret River over the Easter break."

"Well, it's a small world isn't it."

Annie didn't notice Todd's pallor or silence.

"Freya's come to live with us for a while, Todd. I'm going to be a grandmother, and Bronte is going to be a very young auntie. We're getting ready for the baby to arrive in January."

Todd shifted from one foot to the other, restless, then excused himself.

"I just remembered I have to go see someone," Todd choked out. "Nice to see you all."

The batteries could wait.

Millie, please, please be home. He knocked on the back door, only sales reps and 'religious callers' used Millie's front door.

"Todd! Come in." She saw his agitation. "Are you all right?"

"No. Oh, God … no, what have I done?"

They walked into the kitchen and sat at the table. He gulped a deep breath, grasping at his hands and fingers as he grappled with the enormity of what he was about to say.

"I think I'm going to be a father."

"Really?"

Calm and unruffled, Millie invited him to have the discussion he wanted. Todd explained the situation to the wise woman, he trusted her implicitly and knew she would be discrete with what he told her. He was neither ready to take on the responsibility of fatherhood nor marriage to a girl he hardly knew.

"A one-night stand can end in pregnancy, but can you be sure it's your baby? There may well be someone else who could be the father of this child, Todd. Just because Freya is Annie's daughter doesn't mean she holds to the same moral code as her mother."

Little did Millie know that Annie had fallen pregnant with Freya at sixteen. Her parents were ashamed, and kicked her out of their home. She had nowhere to go and no-one to turn to, not even her boyfriend, who didn't want to know her after she told him the news. The Salvation Army introduced her to a widowed Christian woman who gave Annie a home, took her under her wing and helped right through to the birth of the baby. She was a support to Annie and became 'Grandma Delia' to Freya after she was born. They still kept in touch. It's where Annie learned of God's grace and found her faith in Him.

"I don't want to tell Mum and Dad, at least not yet. I think they'd be understanding even though they'd be disappointed and hurt. Mum would probably rush out and buy baby clothes."

They both smiled at this, agreeing it's what she would do.

"What should I do, Millie? I'm just not sure. Should I speak to Freya about it?"

"Firstly, as always, we pray. Then we wait for God's leading."

Todd knew she would say that, and knew it was the right thing to do. They did pray, together, for quite a long time. He was still upset but felt relieved to have someone to talk to about it. The sick feeling in his gut didn't go away and the 'what if' thoughts in his head continued to challenge him.

"Thanks, Millie. I knew you'd understand."

Millie was intrigued by his comment.

The phone rang, and Courtney put the paint roller back in the tray. Three pips sounded in her ear when she picked up the handset. It was a long-distance call, she smiled and checked her watch.

"Hello." Liam spoke first.

"Hi, you're home early."

"The traffic was light today. I've been frustrated with the hold-ups here in the city since being in Mt Barker. No bumper to bumper queues there, hey?"

"No. I've been thinking I should buy a car, it's been a while since I've done any driving but I thought you could give me some more lessons when you get back. What do you think?"

"Great idea, and you'll be fine. Driving is a bit like riding a bike, once you know how to do it you don't forget. You might be a bit rusty at first, but after learning to drive in Sydney it'll be a breeze over there."

Liam remembered the trauma of Courtney's first attempts with L plates in the big city.

"I've been painting the bedroom, and it looks lovely. I chose a duck-egg blue for the walls."

"Nice. Did you order the carpet?"

"Yes."

Their conversation was brief, having shorter calls more often because of the expense. They missed each other with the thousands of kilometres separating them. The guest house was quiet. Jerry and Kate had finished their contract with Keith, and the Tourist Bureau hadn't requested any accommodation for weeks.

After hanging up, Courtney went back to her painting. She recalled the discussion they'd had not long ago.

"I need to talk to you about where I'll live when I come back," Liam broached the subject he'd been mulling over.

"You can stay here, of course."

"But … I don't know, are you sure you're okay with that?"

"Yes," Courtney responded quietly. "What are you really asking, Liam?"

"Well, we are married and I … oh, I don't know."

He struggled with his meaning, and he was usually sure about what he thought and felt.

"Are you talking about sharing a bedroom?"

"I suppose I am, but I don't want to pressure you into anything you don't want to do yet. I've been thinking that maybe we could plan a honeymoon somewhere when you're ready."

He released a sigh. Courtney's heart skipped a beat, he didn't understand how ready she was and it was time to be honest with him.

"What about we have our honeymoon here?"

"At your place?"

"Yes. I don't want to go anywhere else."

"All right."

Relief flooded over him, and he thanked the Lord for answered prayer.

Courtney had decided to freshen up the room to make it their own haven while Liam was away. The bold patterns and colours of wallpaper samples didn't appeal to her, so she chose paint instead. Todd helped dismantle the bed and shift the furniture. He showed her how to cut in around the windows and doors with a paintbrush and the best way to use the roller. Then left her to it.

A new light fitting had been installed by the electrician, and curtains were being made to match the floral quilt she'd chosen. It was going to look fabulous when it all came together. Courtney was sure Liam would like it, especially the creamy coloured shag-pile carpet. That had been an easy decision. Todd suggested polishing the jarrah floor but after having to get out of bed onto cold boards all her life, Courtney wanted the warmth of carpet underfoot. She was going to keep Uncle Geoff's bedroom suite but replace the mattress. It was only two weeks to Christmas and Liam would arrive soon, it would be ready in time.

Freya lounged in the sunshine reading a magazine, her hair shone gold atop her tanned face. Annie watched her from the kitchen window wrestling with the thoughts that had plagued her since her daughter arrived on their doorstep several days ago.

At least she's two years older than I was, but it's not what I wanted for her, Lord. I tried to be a good mother to her and here she is caught in the same situation. I will support her, but Freya doesn't seem perturbed by the responsibility she has to face. She doesn't even know who the father is ... and doesn't care.

Tom came in behind her and placed his arms around her waist.

"I know what you're thinking."

"Do you just?" Annie smiled, he probably did too. He knew her well.

"We'll help her, but I have to say we're not going to molly-coddle her. Freya has to be an active part of this family, and she has to pitch in too. She's pregnant, not sick, Annie." His wife nodded, he was right, Freya had done nothing but laze around all day. A battle was on the horizon, she felt sure of it.

CHAPTER 22

Keith sped up the gravel driveway churning dust out behind him. He pulled up at the big house, jumped out of the ute and went to knock on the door. Annie saw him from the front window as she picked up the phone and waved for him to come in.

"Mum, can you come and get me?"

"Where are you, Freya?"

Annie noticed Keith visibly relax at the question.

"In Mt Barker."

"How did you get into town?"

She had no idea her daughter had even left the house after helping her to bring in the washing. Keith pointed at himself with a guilty look on his face.

"I asked Keith to take me when he was leaving after lunch."

"Just give me a minute," Annie put her hand over the base of the phone and looked at Keith.

"Sorry, Annie, I didn't know she hadn't told you. I looked everywhere for her when she didn't turn up at the post office. I thought she might've found another way back to the vineyard. That's why I rushed home, to make sure she was all right."

Annie nodded, and returned to the phone conversation.

"Where shall I pick you up from?" There was a pause before Freya answered.

"At the police station," was the subdued response.

Annie sighed, annoyed; and closed her eyes in frustration.

"I'll be there soon." Annie hung up.

"Is she at the hospital? She's not having the baby is she? I didn't think she was due yet."

"It's all right, Keith, she's not in hospital. You haven't done anything wrong. Look, I'll have to go and get her. Bronte went out on the tractor with her dad and they won't be back for a little while yet, but the boys will already be on the bus from school. Would you mind waiting for them?"

"No, you go, I'll stay here until either you or Tom get back."

What has she done now? Annie couldn't believe this was happening again, and Freya had only been home for a week. The school bus went by in the opposite direction. Two little faces looked out the back window and watched their mum's car go by. Jimmy and Jon walked into the house to see Keith cutting up apples and cheese to put on a plate with some biscuits. He looked funny doing that kind of thing, they'd never seen him working in the kitchen before.

"Where's Mum gone?" Jon asked.

"To get Freya."

"Where is she?" Jimmy wanted to know.

"In Barker."

"Oh, how come?"

"Don't know. Come and have your afternoon tea now boys. Do you want some milk or water?" Keith made himself a strong cup of coffee and sat at the table, silent. The twins looked at each other and shrugged their shoulders. Adults were weird sometimes and nothing had been the same since Freya had come back to live with them.

Annie parked in a bay close to the entrance door of the station. She braced herself and marched up to the front counter. The sad and sorry looking young lady sat at a desk nearby. Paperwork for her release was signed and they exited the building without saying a word.

"Mum, I'm sorry."

Freya looked across at her mother.

"Do you want to explain yourself?"

"I got caught with someone who was in possession of marijuana."

"Were you buying it?"

"Yes, but they let me off because of my condition, and I didn't actually have the packet in my hands even though I'd given him the money for it."

"Oh, Freya, when are you going to learn? You shouldn't be using that stuff while you're pregnant anyway."

Annie had tears in her eyes, and knew there was no use ranting and raving at her daughter. All she could do was keep praying, and let God deal with her.

"Will you tell Tom?"

It was apparent Freya didn't want him to know what had happened.

"No, but I think you should. He'll probably hear about it from someone else if you don't." Annie couldn't believe how lenient the Sergeant had been. They drove past the Old Police Station Museum[5] on their way home and she thought Freya should be very thankful she wasn't back in those early days.

Todd was on Millie's doorstep again, she pushed the flyscreen door open and welcomed him. He'd lost weight and didn't wear his usual smile, concern for him filled Millie with sadness. His plight was wearing on him.

"How's it going, Todd?"

She asked the leading question to give him permission to spill his thoughts and feelings in her presence. This was the third visit in two weeks.

"I keep getting that Bible verse in Psalms to wait for the Lord but its wearing me down. How am I supposed to find out anything if I have to sit tight and wait?"

"Sometimes that's God's way, Todd. Are you trusting this is the answer to your prayer?"

"Yes, I know in my heart it is, but my head keeps fighting with it."

Millie got her Bible out and opened it up at the Psalms.

"What was that reference again?"

---

5 Old Police Station Museum

"Psalm 27:14," Todd told her, "I know it by heart now. 'Wait patiently for the Lord. Be strong and courageous. Yes, wait for the Lord.' But waiting is killing me, what am I waiting for? I don't do patience well, Millie. Maybe it's being strong enough to have courage to do *nothing*. What do you think?"

"I think you need to remember to trust in the Lord, and not depend on your own understanding ..." she flipped the pages through to Proverbs Chapter 3.

"Yeah, I know, and acknowledge God ... in all my ways ..."

"... and He will show you what to do. Trust and wait, Todd, and as difficult as it is, it's the only way to relinquish your anxiety. God wouldn't expect you to go through this without there being a plan in it. Just wait, I know you can do it."

Millie's encouragement helped, his step was lighter as he walked down the driveway to his ute.

CHAPTER 23

U ncle Geoff's diary sat open on the coffee table in the lounge room. His account of meeting Matilda had piqued Courtney's interest amid the writing of his work and notes on significant scripture passages and verses. The phone rang.

"Liam, I found some interesting notes in one of Uncle Geoff's diaries. They're personal – about him and Matilda. I noticed a mark next to the first one, and as I flipped through the other pages I found more entries about Matilda with the same marking. These pages look well-worn. I wonder if he read and re-read them over the years." Courtney hoped Liam was as interested in this as she was.

"Read it to me, I don't want to wait until next week." He was due to arrive on Sunday, three days before Christmas. "It doesn't matter if our phone call's a bit longer today."

"Okay, I'll start with the first one he wrote."

* 'Today, I was in a hurry for an appointment in St George's Terrace, and I rushed through London Court from Hay Street. It wasn't easy with street stalls, window shoppers and banners strung out along the narrow cobbled lane. In my haste, I bumped into an

elderly man, a minister-of-the-cloth. I turned to apologise, and I noticed the young woman on his arm. Our eyes met, and her father saw the lingering look we shared. He held up his hand and said, "It's all right, son, no harm done." She'd nudged him with her elbow. "This is my daughter, Matilda." I introduced myself, but had to be on my way. I'd never believed in love at first sight. I think differently now.'

"Then there's this one a few pages further on."

* 'I went to St Andrew's Presbyterian Church in the city tonight. The choral recital was magnificent, and as I scanned the faces of the singers I saw her. Matilda. She took my breath away, her face glowed with love for the Lord. I ventured to approach her at the supper table. She remembered me, and we had a lovely chat. I have her address, and she's happy for me to call on her.'

"There are several one sentence notes about things they did together. And, I found this bit about the locket. You remember, the one I showed you?"

"Yes, I remember it. What does the diary say?"

* 'It's Matilda's birthday today. I collected a gold locket from the jewellers. Our names are engraved on the back, and I cut out our tiny faces from a photograph to

put inside it. I hope she'll love it.'

"I didn't remember seeing the names, so I went and got it out of the box. They are there, but only faint. I guess it was worn down from rubbing against Matilda's clothing when she wore it. She can't have taken it off very often."

"I guess she liked it then, hey?"

"Yes, I'd say so, but Liam, it takes a bad turn a few months later. Shall I keep going?"

"Yeah, don't leave me in the lurch now."

* *'My heart is breaking, and I don't understand why this has to be. We are all believers, same God, same truth, same faith. Why should denomination matter? We love each other, isn't that enough? We can overcome the few doctrinal differences, Lord, surely we could. Why does her father have to be so dogmatic about this?'*

"And then, the bombshell ..."

* *'I received a letter from Matilda's father today. He apologised for the hurt his separating us will cause but because I was baptised a Catholic as an infant he won't agree to my proposal of marriage to Matilda. She will honour her father's wishes as she's been raised to do. I am defeated, I will never love again, my Matilda is lost to me. Help me, please Lord, to lean on you.'*

"I feel so sad for him, but I can see the lovely man Uncle Geoff was. Poor fellow, it was so unfair and he never stopped loving her. It was worth trawling through all those other pages just to find this treasure. I've only got one more book to go, and I will have read them all. I like the notes on the Bible verses, I've learned a lot from them. He was a deep thinker, and trusted God implicitly. I hope I can be like him one day."

"So do I." Then Liam quickly added, "Me, I mean."

At 6.00am in Sydney, one week before Christmas, Liam drove out of the city limits and headed west. The long haul to cover 4,000 kilometres had begun. It would take at least four days. He felt the covering of prayer from his loved ones while on the journey.

He was excited about the prospect of returning to Western Australia. His furniture was stored in his parent's garage, a few things were already being trucked over and would arrive before him. He was going to take most of his clothing and precious things packed in suitcases and boxes when he drove across in his car. He'd said farewell to family and friends at a special dinner held at his Mum and Dad's house.

Huge trucks going east and west were the main vehicles on the roads. Wombats, kangaroos and wedge-tailed eagles were scattered along the way as road kill. Warning signs for camels were a surprise to him, and he saw several emus. Salty bore-water showers at the roadhouses when he ventured across the Nullabor left him feeling sticky and less clean than before washing off the sweat from the long, hot December days.

Heat haze mirages on the never-ending straight roads were something he hadn't seen before. His life was a myriad of new experiences. Liam had to pull over when the sun began to set on the western horizon, it was impossible to see anything with it blazing right in his eyes. For two days he'd slept for a few hours in the middle of the day, and drove in the cooler evening. Most of the roadhouses were open for 24 hours and he could refuel and restock his food supply.

"I'm in WA," Liam announced proudly when he rang Courtney. "I thought I'd wait until I got to Eucla before I called you. We're in the same time zone now, but this pay phone is still going to chew up my coins quickly. I'll be heading for Norseman tomorrow. That's about 700 kilometres to cover, and there are five roadhouses along the way, so it'll be an easy stretch."

Courtney was horrified at the idea, not realising the distances Liam had already covered along the vast Nullabor Plain.

"I had no idea how huge our country was until I started this trek. It's so flat and red and scrubby. I had a chat to some people who'd driven from Albany using the road between Hyden and Norseman. They said it was in good condition, and even though it's gravel and dusty, it's much quicker than going through Kalgoorlie or Esperance. I was warned it's very hot and to carry plenty of water. I wouldn't imagine its any hotter than here, although it'll be drier because it's inland. This road I'm on now isn't too far from the coast along the Great Australian Bight. Anyway, I'm going to check with the contact number they gave me to see if it's open when I get there."

"Don't take any risks, Liam. I want you here safe and sound."

"No, I won't, and from Hyden it's mostly bitumen roads through the wheat belt. The farmers are harvesting their grain, so that'll be interesting to see. I'm looking forward to it."

"I got a message for you from the truck depot. Your stuff's arrived, and they said to pick it up whenever you're ready. There's no hurry, though."

"Great. I gotta go, there's this girl I'm going to see, and I have to get back on the road," he chuckled at his own humour. Courtney was pleased it wouldn't be long before he arrived. She had to admit she'd been concerned about him driving all that way alone."

CHAPTER 24

Back and forth, back and forth, the locket slid along the chain between Courtney's thumb and finger. She'd been to the window several times while waiting anxiously for Liam to arrive. He'd rung to say he was at Amelup, east of the Stirling Ranges, just over an hour away. She decided to sit on the front verandah instead of pacing in the kitchen.

Liam drove along Lancaster Road, and tooted the horn as he came in the driveway. Courtney flew down the front steps to meet him. She threw her arms around him as soon as he got out of the car, and held him tight.

"You're here at last," she whispered. *Thank you, Lord.*

Liam kissed the top of her head, her eyes, nose, and cheeks. Their lips met in a long, lingering kiss. They picked up a case each and headed inside. The other luggage could wait.

"Welcome home."

"It does feel like home, our home."

The suitcases were put down in the kitchen, and Liam had a long drink of water.

"Show me this renovated room, Courtney, I'm dying to see it."

"Close your eyes."

He held her hand, and let her lead him to the doorway in the passage.

"Okay, open them." He nodded as his eyes glanced around the room.

"I'm impressed. You've done a great job. I love that carpet." Liam ran his hand through the soft cream-coloured shag-pile. Courtney beamed at his comments, but noticed the lines around his tired eyes. He was worn out.

"Do you need to have a rest?"

"You know what I want? A bath, a bite to eat and bed, in that order."

"Coming right up." She ran a warm bath, and while Liam soaked his weary bones she made some ham and cheese toasted sandwiches.

"That feels better already."

Their conversation shifted at Liam's next comment.

"I've applied for a job in Mt Barker."

"Really. Where? Doing what?"

"Teaching. A friend of mine put me onto an advert for a Maths teacher at the Mt Barker District High School. So I've applied for it, and now I have to wait and see whether or not I get it."

"But you hate teaching maths."

"Not that much, a job is a job, and a chance to teach Social Studies or History might come up in the future. I'll be with you, and that's what matters most."

"Aw," Courtney feigned being mushy, but she was touched by his comment.

She'd heard about the first school teacher in Mt Barker and because of Liam's love of history, she knew he'd want to know the details.[6] She shared a brief version of it and promised to tell him all about it later because he'd yawned several times, even though it was only early afternoon.

"Off to bed for you now, and have a good sleep." Courtney tucked him in and kissed his forehead. He fell asleep straight away.

Courtney woke up beside Liam's warm body in bed the next morning. He was still asleep. She reached over to push back a lock of wavy brown hair away from his face. My precious husband. Thank you for him, Lord, and for bringing him safely to me. Her touch disturbed him, and he opened his sleep heavy eyes. A smile played on his lips.

"Now this is what I've been waiting for, to wake up beside you. And, I will be every day from now on." His husky voice and open arms lured her into his embrace.

Christmas plans had been put in place. They were to spend Christmas Eve with Millie and then head out to Frankland after the 9.00 o'clock church service for Christmas lunch with Keith and the O'Reilly family. Food preparations were underway, and Courtney felt an excitement she'd never known before. She removed a hot tray of star-shaped gingerbread biscuits from the oven when Liam came up behind her

---

6 Mt Barker schools

and slid his arms around her waist. The biscuits nearly went flying when she jumped at his touch.

"Oops, sorry. I shouldn't have done that, but I couldn't resist."

"It's okay." She turned in his arms, and they shared a quick kiss.

"I've got to keep cooking. There's a lot to get ready today."

Liam noticed the locket, and lifted it to have a closer look.

"Were you wearing this yesterday?"

"Yes."

"I thought so. It's Matilda's isn't it?"

"Yes."

"That's nice. Does it have their photo's inside?"

"Yes."

"Can I have a look?"

"Yes."

"Do you love me like Uncle Geoff loved Matilda?"

"Yes." She smiled knowing he was cashing in on the yes answers. "I thought it would've pleased him to know I was wearing it."

"I'm sure of it. They were a handsome couple, weren't they?"

"Yes."

"Just like us."

Courtney giggled. He was being a pest, and she was busy.

"Go and unpack your stuff, and let me get on with my jobs."

Millie came bearing gifts on Christmas Eve, the threesome enjoyed a light meal together and swapped presents afterwards. Courtney couldn't help but smile at the pleasure of enjoying a real Christmas. It was a lovely evening, and the young couple radiated their happiness. Millie was sure they were destined to be together. God does work in mysterious ways, she thought. She loved the beautiful Swarovski crystal waterlily candle-holder that Courtney and Liam had given her. It would take pride of place on her sideboard. Liam walked her to the gate when it was time to go home.

"I can't thank you enough, Millie, for all you've done for Courtney."

"Think nothing of it, Liam. I was always going to be there for her. She's been a part of my life too, admittedly second-hand, through Geoffrey. I couldn't love her more if she was my own flesh and blood. I can't tell you how much it pleases me to see you two together. It's been an answer to prayer, and a blessing to me as well. God bless you, son. Goodnight."

A slight slump of her shoulders went unnoticed, and Millie toddled off to her back door. Liam watched her go until the porch light was turned off. He shook his head, what a gem she is, he thought.

"Liam, Li-am ..." Courtney bounced on the bed. "Come on, wake up, it's Christmas."

A groan emanated from the waking soul who couldn't disguise his pleasure at her wake-up call. Several gifts jiggled up and down beside him. He looked at the bedside clock, it was only 6.00am.

"You're as bad as a little child."

"I know, it's such fun. Come on, open your presents."

"This one first," she handed him a small square box.

Liam unwrapped it.

"Nice, a Swatch watch. I like it." He put it on and gave her a hug.

"Now this one."

"How many presents did you buy? One should be enough."

"I wanted to spoil you."

He found two T-shirts, a denim jacket and a light blue button-through shirt with a navy blue and tan paisley tie.

"You can wear those to church this morning." Courtney announced.

"Yes, Ma'am." Liam grabbed her and tickled her until she could barely breathe. "Now it's my turn."

He jumped off the bed and went to the tree in the lounge room to pick up his gifts for her.

"I thought you said one present was enough." She smiled as he handed her the neatly wrapped boxes.

"Happy first Christmas together, sweetheart." He gave her a cassette player with music tapes by Amy Grant and Twila Paris; a Rubik's cube, and a bottle of No. 4711 Eau de Cologne. They ate breakfast in bed, and Liam messed up the coloured squares on the cube. They kept turning the rows back and forth. Only one side was nearly all red, and the rest were still muddled up. Courtney was stumped about how to solve it.

Massive flower arrangements adorned the church, and a happy atmosphere pervaded the building. Merry Christmas echoed in harmony as people greeted each other while they took their seats. Reverend Bob welcomed the congregation, and the pianist played the Ode to Joy. Everyone joined in with the words: Joy to the world, the Lord is come. Let earth receive her King, let every heart prepare Him room … Annie, Tom and the children came in on the last strains of the final verse, and sat in the front row. It was the only pew left with enough room for them all.

Christmas carols resounded with gusto, and the choir sang a cantata of Angels from the realms of Glory. Reverend Bob delivered a message of hope and encouraged worship of Christ the newborn King. Everyone had a quick chat outside in the sunshine after the service before rushing off to check the food in their ovens.

Millie was standing with the York's when Annie came over to announce Freya had delivered her baby just before midnight last night, on Christmas Eve.

"It's a girl, and she doesn't look anything like her mother. She weighs a healthy 7lbs 2oz, and there were no complications." Annie had been with her daughter throughout the birth.

"Freya doesn't have a name for her yet, but the kids have a heap of suggestions." The hospital had given Annie a Polaroid photo of the newborn to show family and friends. David and Helen cooed over the baby snap, and congratulated the new grandmother then passed the photo to Todd. He took a nervous look at the little girl, and tears stung at the back of his eyes.

"She's beautiful, Annie. Congratulations." He gave the photo to Millie and strode away from the group. She watched him go before she took a look at the picture, and then understood his reaction. After a genuine polite response she excused herself, and let Helen know she'd see her in about an hour at their place with the pudding and brandy butter for dessert.

Todd stood over by the entrance gates. He knew Millie would come.

"I can't believe it, Millie. Now I know why God said to wait. That baby is definitely not mine. I'm relieved, and I dread to think of the mess I would've made if I'd barged in … it would have been a disastrous mistake." The image of the dark olive-skinned baby wrapped in a pretty pink blanket with her jet black hair, little flat nose and almond-shaped eyes peeking out were all Hawaiian traits. His countenance lightened, and he breathed easier than he had done in weeks.

"I've met him, the Hawaiian guy that's probably the father. They call him 'Tackay' because he uses a Donald Takayama surfboard. He travels around the world from one surf break to the next. The girls all moon over him, and the guys are jealous of his good looks and incredible surfing skills. I'd seen him in Indonesia, and he'd already been in Margaret River for a month before I went there."

"We can praise God there are no question marks about the baby's parentage now, and no need for blood tests or sticky situations. It took courage for you to wait, Todd, and your obedience has resolved this in a way you didn't expect."

"Can we thank God together?"

"Of course we can." They prayed for Freya and the baby, too.

"I can't wait to get stuck into that turkey. I'm so hungry. Mum will be pleased. She's been suspicious that something wasn't right. Now we can all relax and enjoy Christmas Day."

CHAPTER 25

Courtney sang as they packed away the baubles from the Christmas tree. "Dashing through the snow on a one-horse open sleigh, over the fields we go laughing all the way ..." When she finished the verse Liam started to sing the chorus.

"Jingle bells, Batman smells, Robin flew away, Father Christmas lost his whiskers flying TAA."

"Weren't the twins funny when we sang that?"

"They thought it was hilarious." Liam had been surprised they hadn't heard it before. "And they had no idea about what Trans-Atlantic Airways were."

"It was a great day. I haven't had a Christmas like it before."

Courtney loved every moment of the family celebration.

The doorbell rang.

A tall man wearing an Akubra and sunglasses smiled when Courtney opened the door.

"Hello," she greeted and recognised him when he removed his glasses. "Oh, it's you Jarvo. Come on in," Courtney invited.

"Sorry, I can't stay. I'm heading into Albany to pick up my son and daughter from the bus. They're arriving from Bunbury this afternoon."

Liam came to the door and Courtney introduced them.

"Liam, this is Jarvo."

"Hi. Nice to meet you." Liam noticed the unusual colour of the man's eyes.

"My last visit was a rescue mission. I was stuck, and Courtney helped me out with a night's accommodation. That's why I'm here. I was wondering if I might be able to book in for an extended stay."

"Extended? As in how long?"

"Well, I'm hoping we might be able to stay for the two weeks of swimming lessons. They start at the pool on Monday 5ᵗʰ January and go til Friday the following week. We would go home to the farm for the weekend in between."

Courtney looked to Liam for confirmation. He nodded his ascent, waved to Jarvo and retreated to the lounge room to continue tidying up. Courtney closed the door behind her and moved onto the verandah. She considered the logistics.

"Okay, we have Jerry and Kate coming for New Year's, but they'll be gone before then. I don't see it will be a problem. Two children, you say. We could put a couple of fold-up beds in the guest wing. Would that be all right?"

"Perfect. I decided to treat the kids with a bit of a holiday. They usually do their swimming lessons in Bunbury. They had Christmas with their Nanna and Pop, but Pop's had a turn with his heart. It's far too much to expect the children to stay over there this year."

"We'll be delighted to have you. Are there any foods you or your family don't like? If I know what it is, I won't cook it."

"You'll do the cooking?"

"Yes, you get breakfast and dinner. Not lunches though."

"Great, I'll get to have a holiday as well. Wonderful, the kids are pretty good, they eat anything."

"We'll look forward to having you all." They discussed the costs, and settled on a fair price for the longer booking. Courtney walked with him down the steps to the path.

Millie was out in her front garden watering the ferns under the big tree. It was a warm day, and she was enjoying being outside. Voices from Courtney's front yard caught her attention. She looked across to see a man leaving, his loping stride had a familiar gait, but she didn't know who it was. Courtney called over to ask her to come for a cuppa.

Liam shifted the diaries from the fireplace mantle to return them to the coffee table, but one of them got caught on the corner of the ledge, and he dropped it. A yellowed newspaper clipping fell out onto the floor. Liam picked it up and read it. He was shocked by what he saw. The image painted a very real picture of the accident, and the text explained the event.

He didn't want Courtney to see this, not today. She was happy. They already had enough to deal with as it was. In a few days it would be their first New Year's Eve together, and they had to make the time of the year a happy occasion instead of being clouded by her past experience. Liam decided to take the article and put it in his bedside drawer under some other paperwork. He'd wait to share it with her, and he would pray about the right time for that to happen, too.

Millie and Courtney had just got to the top of the stairs when they heard a car horn toot. A red ute pulled into the driveway and Todd jumped out. He often called in on Sunday afternoons to visit after he'd been to church in Albany.

"Hello," the women said in unison.

"I'll go and make some coffee, and let Liam know you're here."

Courtney went to go inside, but Liam was already there.

"How could I not know he was here with all that racket going on?" Liam reached out and shook hands with Todd. "Hi," he turned to Millie, "I didn't realise you were here as well," and he gave her a hug.

They sat on the front verandah enjoying the sunshine, and each other's company. Courtney brought out some Brasso, and a rag, to polish the brass lion emblem on the front door.

"I've been meaning to do this for ages," she said as the cleaning fluid began to remove the oxidisation from the brass surface. "That looks better." It soon shone bright and clean.

"Your roses are stunning this summer, Courtney." Millie was impressed.

"I've been doing all the things Maureen said to do, and it's paid off."

"The scent is beautiful. It's a bit sad they only have one show of flowers each season," Millie lamented.

"Oh, really, I didn't know."

"Mmm, the red one is an old gallic rose. It was used for medicine in the old days, and perfumes were made from it too."

"Roses have names, don't they? What are they called?" Liam asked.

"The red one is the Lancaster Rose, and the white one is the York Rose." Millie obliged.

Todd and Courtney were surprised to discover they bore their surnames.

Liam sat still, then threw his head back and laughed out loud. Everyone looked at him as if he was weird.

"What's so funny?" Todd wanted to share in the joke.

"Lancaster, York, the Plantagenet's, the Wars of the Roses! Don't you know your historical roots?" Liam continued to chuckle. "Well, I never ..." he went on to explain with a history lesson for their benefit.

"Did you know the emblem on the door is from the Coat of Arms of the Royal House of Plantagenet?"

"No, I thought it was something to do with Plantagenet Wines," Courtney offered.

"The Plantagenet family line goes right back to the 1100's. And you're going to love this -

Empress *Matilda*, daughter of King Henry I, married *Geoffrey* of Anjou after her first husband died. She was in line for the throne, but because she was a woman they wouldn't accept her. She was never crowned Queen but was given a title: The Lady of the English. She, and her brother Robert, were commissioned to protect the south-west of England. Geoffrey conquered Normandy, and Matilda moved to Rouen in France while her eldest son succeeded to the throne as Henry II in 1154. She worked with the church in France, and was involved in developing monastries for Roman Catholic monks and nuns. Matilda is buried under the high altar in Bec Abbey in Normandy."

"Whew, that's a lot of information to absorb. I'm glad I chose to study geography at school," Todd commented after Liam finished his explanation.

"What about the Wars of the Roses?" Courtney wanted to know.

"It's probably all a bit boring. Are you sure you want to hear more?"

"Yes," all three voices in the audience chimed in together.

"Briefly, the wars, and there were many of them, occurred in the mid-1400's when Henry VI was mentally unstable. He didn't produce an heir with his wife, Margaret of Anjou, until many years later. In the meantime, Richard of York manipulated his position to be Lord Protector and Chief Regent while Henry was unwell. The York and Lancaster factions battled it out over the years for supremacy and the crown. Double-crossing and treachery between rival family members sparked most of the conflict."

"So, that explains a lot then." Todd commented.

"About what?" Liam queried.

"Why Courtney and I were often at loggerheads with each other when we first met."

They all had a laugh about that.

"The defining conflict was the Battle of Bosworth Field in 1485. Henry Tudor victoriously fought Richard III on 22 August, where Richard died, and Tudor was crowned King Henry VII. Henry married Elizabeth of York, and united the York and Lancaster families to establish the beginning of the Tudor Dynasty. The Tudor Rose was created by combining the red and the white roses to symbolise the end of the Wars of the Roses."

"The York's and the Lancaster's, how about that? Our heritage is important, isn't it?" Courtney directed her query to Liam.

"Yes, that's why history records births and deaths, and family lines for generations. Even the Old Testament has lists of 'so-and-so begat someone' for pages at a time, but it can be a bit of a trial reading through it all."

"And, don't forget Jesus' genealogy is recorded in the New Testament," Millie added. "What I love is that we are all part of God's family. Christmas reminded me, again, of the value of God's gift to all of us. We are his heirs together, and we share a common bond in our Saviour." Her eyes drifted toward the heavens, and she wiped a single tear aside before anyone could notice it.

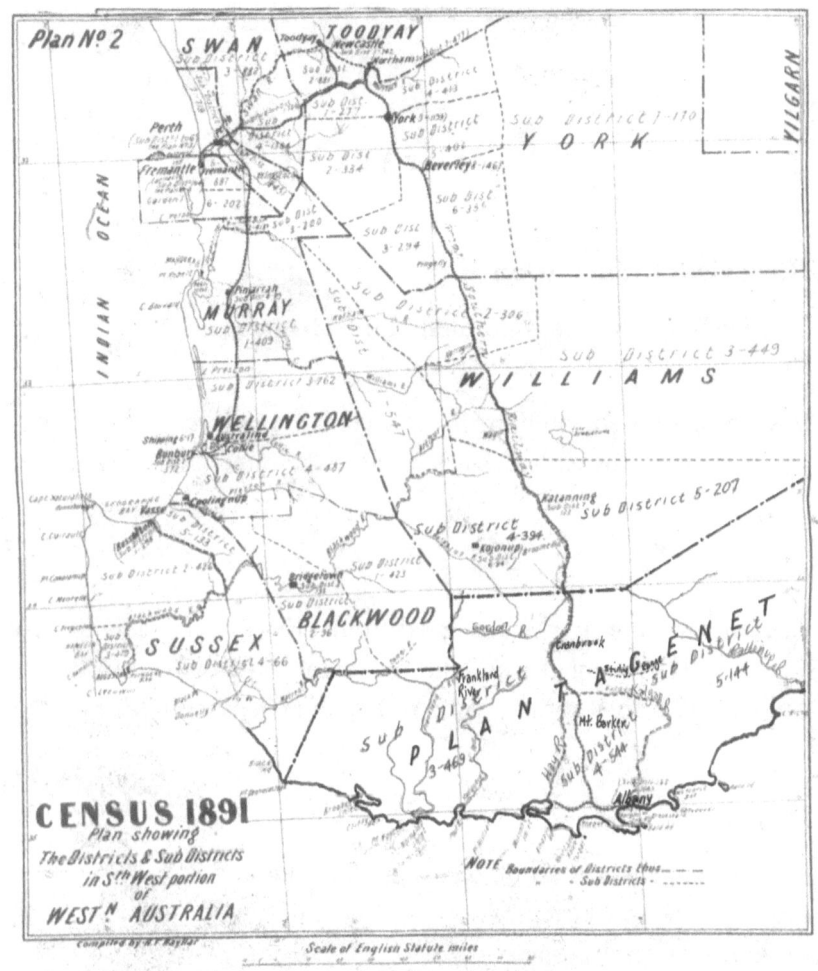

**PLANTAGENET DISTRICT IN WESTERN AUSTRALIA
AS AT CENSUS 1891**

AFTERWORD

Historical Information

The Plantagenet Shire is located in the Great Southern of Western Australia.

It is a rural shire surrounding the town of Mount Barker, near Albany, and was named by early English settlers who often used royal titles.

Plantagenet (n.)

English royal house which reigned from 1154 to 1485 (Henry II to Richard III), emerged from the nickname of Geoffrey, Count of Anjou, who wore a sprig of broom, L. planta genista, in his cap.

Planta genista – linifolia

An erect narrow-leaf shrub bearing yellow flowers
Prolific in the south-west of Western Australia
Introduced from Europe in the 1800's

Footnote references:

1. **Mt Barker** is known for Plantagenet Wines and the spectacular wildflowers of the Porongorup and Stirling Ranges. In 1829, while the Governor Phillip was in King George Sound for repairs ship surgeon, Thomas Braidwood Wilson, explored the inland area from Albany

with Noongar guide Mokare. The hill, known as 'Pwakkenbak' to the local indigenous tribe was named after Captain Collet Barker, the commandant of the garrison at King George Sound at the time.

2. **All Saints Anglican Church** boasts Gothic-arch stained glass windows depicting biblical scenes which can be appreciated from inside. Outside, the windows are decorated with white rendered surrounds. Red painted double wooden Gothic-style doors announce a welcome entry into the pleasant interior. It was a stone chancel built in 1900 where a foundation stone was laid by Mrs BH Wright. She was the granddaughter of the Reverend M Mitchell, who was a pioneer clergyman of the diocese. It was consecrated by the Lord Bishop on 15 December of that year. In 1926, the brick nave was built on to the original building.

3. **The Old Bush Inn** provided a place for settlers, shepherds and ticket-of-leave men employed on farms in the Plantagenet district to get together. It was established in 1860 by William C. Cooper who obtained a licence from the Government Resident in Albany to commence business as a publican. The three roomed cottage served as a resting place and the Royal Mail coaches changed horses between Albany and Kojonup. For a long time it was the only building in Mt Barker and within nine years Cooper had expanded his public house. The Plantagenet Road Board met there in April, 1871, and accommodated government officials including Governor Frederick Weld. The Inn benefited from the Royal Mail passenger service from Albany to Perth from 1880. The railway station opened in 1899, delivering mail and transporting passengers. The Park Hotel

was established in 1914, and the Old Bush Inn permanently closed its doors.

4. **Mt Frankland,** or **'Caldyanup'** to the local Aboriginal people, is a steep granite outcrop with stunning views. The region has a beauty of its own where tall Karri trees create a towering canopy. Rangers and fire-spotters use the peak as an outlook during summer seasons. Mt Lindsay, Mt Roe and the Walpole Wilderness area are all visible from there. Wildflowers bloom in the spring bringing the grey-greens of the natural bush into an array of colour growing along the hiking trails.

5. **Old Police Station Museum** Mt Barker's first policeman, Constable Daniel O'Connell lived at the Old Police Station built by convicts in 1867. It was officially opened on 6th March, 1868. Before a lock-up was added to the side of the stables in 1887, the constable tied his prisoner to a log in front of the station during the day. If a prisoner was in custody overnight, the constable's family moved out of the kitchen and the detainee was secured to the leg of the table. The following morning the prisoner would be transported to Albany.

6. **Mt Barker Schools** Miss Francis Mitchell, from Albany, was appointed teacher of 30 students in 1893. The classes were held in the original Plantagenet Hall, a small wooden building relocated from Torbay. In February 1894, the school moved to an ironstone building on the Perth Road, now Albany Highway. Church services were held there for a time. Miss Mitchell later married the Postmaster, Mr RH Wright. After WWI there was a growth in population of

young families in the region. More schools were needed to provide education for these students and one-room schools popped up throughout the district. Grades one through to seven were taught by one teacher. Children would walk or ride horses to school. By the 1920's and 1930's transport changed from horses to motorised vehicles and school buses were able to transport children longer distances to a centralised school in Mt Barker. A high school was built in the 1950's to keep families closer in distance than sending their youth to boarding schools in Albany and Perth.

Sources:

Heritage Trail - Mount Barker – Settlement and Development of the Mount Barker District

Rainbow Coast website – Mt Frankland National Park in the Walpole region WA

What We Were – All Saints Church and the Parish of Mount Barker – Nancy Jellico

(http://htawa.net.au/WA-100-years/files/community/Mt-Barker-Plantagenet-Shire-Brief-History-e.pdf)

(http://www.plantagenet.wa.gov.au/)

(https://en.wikipedia.org/wiki/House_of_Plantagenet)

(https://www.britannica.com/topic/house-of-Plantagenet)

(https://florabase.dpaw.wa.gov.au/browse/profile/3936)

COMING SOON...

SETH'S SOLACE
BOOK TWO IN THE PLANTAGENET TRILOGY

A sheep farmer from Cranbrook in the Great Southern of Western Australia thought his life was perfect, until the day he was abandoned. Disillusioned and torn, peace eludes Seth Jarvis. As heart-wrenching trials unfold before him, will he lean on the only one he can truly trust?

Seth negotiates a rocky climb in the search to solve his problems resulting in unavoidable consequences. His new-found friends are left struggling to understand the path he has chosen.

Book Two in the Plantagenet Trilogy continues with the lives and friendships of characters from *Courtney's Keys*. Thought-provoking questions expose unexpected revelations and resolutions. Flourishing new romances develop on the sun-drenched western horizon.

www.ingramcontent.com/pod-product-compliance
Lightning Source LLC
Chambersburg PA
CBHW022144240626
47153CB00007B/2502